JOURNALS OF

OTHER WORKS BY NORMAN SPINRAD

Novels

Agent of Chaos
Bug Jack Barron
Child of Fortune
The Children of Hamelin
Deus X
The Iron Dream
Little Heroes
The Men in the Jungle
The Mind Game
Passing Through the Flame
Pictures at 11
Riding the Torch
Russian Spring
The Solarians
Songs from the Stars
The Void Captain's Tale
A World Between

Story Collections

The Last Hurrah of the Golden Horde
No Direction Home
Other Americas
The Star-Spangled Future

Nonfiction

Fragments of America
Stayin' Alive: A Writer's Guide
Science Fiction in the Real World

Anthologies (editor)

The New Tomorrows
Modern Science Fiction

JOURNALS
of the
PLAGUE YEARS

Norman Spinrad

BANTAM BOOKS

New York   Toronto   London
Sydney   Auckland

JOURNALS OF THE PLAGUE YEARS
A Bantam Spectra Book/September 1995

SPECTRA and the portrayal of a boxed "s" are trademarks of Bantam Books, a division of
Bantam Doubleday Dell Publishing Group, Inc.

BOOK DESIGN BY GLEN M. EDELSTEIN

Library of Congress Cataloging-in-Publication Data
Spinrad, Norman.
    Journals of the plague years / Norman Spinrad.
      p.   cm.
   ISBN 0-553-37399-4
   PS3569.P55J68   1995
813'.54—dc20   94-39704
                                                        CIP
Published simultaneously in the United States and Canada

Bantam Books are published by Bantam Books, a division of Bantam Doubleday Dell
Publishing Group, Inc. Its trademark, consisting of the words "Bantam Books" and the
portrayal of a rooster, is Registered in U.S. Patent and Trademark Office and in other
countries. Marca Registrada. Bantam Books, 1540 Broadway, New York, New York 10036.

PRINTED IN THE UNITED STATES OF AMERICA

FFG 10 9 8 7 6 5 4 3 2 1

In memoriam:

RUUD WICHERTS

LUC ALEXANDER

JOURNALS OF THE PLAGUE YEARS

INTRODUCTION

IT WAS THE WORST OF TIMES, AND IT WAS THE SADDEST OF TIMES, so what we must remember if we are to keep our perspective as we read these journals of the Plague Years is that the people who wrote them, indeed the entire population of what was then the United States of America, and most of the world, were, by our standards, all quite mad.

The Plague virus, apparently originating somewhere in Africa, had spread first to male homosexuals and intravenous drug users. Inevitably it moved via bisexual contact into the population at large. A vaccine was developed and for a moment the Plague seemed defeated. But the organism mutated under this evolutionary pressure and a new strain swept the world. A new vaccine was developed, but the virus mutated again. Eventually the succession of vaccines selected for mutability itself, and the Plague virus, proliferated into dozens of strains.

Palliative treatments were developed—victims might survive for a decade or more—but there was no cure and no vaccine that offered protection for long.

For twenty years, sex and death were inextricably entwined. For twenty years, men and women were constrained to deny themselves the ordinary pleasures of straightforward, unencumbered sex, or to succumb to the natural desires of the flesh and pay the awful price. For twenty years, the species faced its own extinction. For twenty years, Africa and most of Asia and Latin America were quarantined by the armed forces of America, Europe, Japan, and Russia. For twenty years, the people of the world stewed in their own frustrated sexual juices.

Small wonder then that the Plague Years were years of madness. Small wonder that the authors of these journals seem, from our happier perspective, driven creatures, and quite insane.

That each of them found somewhere the courage to carry on, that through their tormented and imperfect instrumentalities the long night was finally to see our dawn, *that* is the wonder, that is the triumph of the human spirit, the spirit that unites the era of the Plague Years with our own.

—Mustapha Kelly
Luna City, 2143

JOHN DAVID

I WAS GUNFODDERING IN BAJA WHEN THE MARKS BEGAN TO APPEAR
again. The first time I saw the marks, they gave me six years
if I could afford it, ten if I joined up and got myself the best.

Well, what was a poor boy to do? Take my black card,
let them stick me in a Quarantine Zone, and take my
chances? Go underground and try to dodge the Sex Police
until the Plague got me? Hell no, this poor boy did what
about two million other poor boys did—he signed up for
life in the American Foreign Legion, aka the Army of the
Living Dead, while he was still in good enough shape to be
accepted.

Now you hear a lot of bad stuff about the Legion. The
wages suck. The food ain't much. We're a bunch of blood-
thirsty killers too bugfuck to be allowed back in the United
States fighting an endless imperialistic war against the whole
Third World, and our combat life expectancy is about three

years. Junkies. Dopers. Drooling sex maniacs. The scum of the universe.

For sure, all that is true. But unless you're a millionaire or supercrook, the Legion is the best deal you can do when they paint your blue card black and tell you you've Got It.

The deal is, you get the latest that medical science has to offer and you get it free. The deal is, you can do anything you want to the gorks as long as you don't screw up combat orders. The deal is that the Army of the Living Dead is coed and omnisexual and every last one of us has already Got It. We've all got our black cards already, we're under sentence of death, so we might as well enjoy one another on the way out. The deal is that the Legion is all the willing meat-sex you can handle, and plenty that you can't, you better believe it!

Like the recruiting slogan says, "A Short Life but a Happy One." We were the last free red-blooded American boys and girls. "Join the Army and Fuck the World," says the graffiti they scrawl on the walls about us.

Well, that too, and so what?

Take the Baja campaign. The last census showed that the black card population of California was entitled to enlarged Quarantine Zones. Catalina and San Francisco were bursting at the seams and the state legislature couldn't agree on a convenient piece of territory. So it got booted up to the Federal Quarantine Agency.

Old Walter T., he looks at the map, and he sees you could maintain a Quarantine line across the top of the Baja Peninsula with maybe two thousand SP troops. Real convenient. Annex the mother to California and solve the problem.

So in we go, and down the length of Baja we cakewalk.

No sweat. Two weeks of saturation air strikes to soften up the Mexes, a heavy armored division and two wings of gunships at the point, followed by fifteen thousand of us zombies to nail things down.

What you call a fun campaign, a far cry from the mess we got into in Cuba or that balls-up in Venezuela, let me tell you. Mexico was something like fifty percent Got It, their armed forces had been wiped out of existence in the Chihuahua campaign, and so it was just a matter of three weeks of leisurely pillage, rape, and plunder.

The Mexes? They got a sweet deal, considering. Those who were still alive by the time we had secured Baja down to La Paz could choose between deportation to what was left of Mexico or becoming black card citizens of the state of California, Americans like thee and me, brothers and sisters. Any one of them who had survived had Gotten It in every available orifice about 150 times by us zombies by then anyway.

Wanna moralize about it? Okay, then moralize this one, meatfucker:

The damn Plague started in Africa, didn't it? That's the Third World, ain't it? Africa, Latin America, Asia, except for China, Japan, and Iran, they're over 50 percent Got It, ain't they? And the It they Got keeps mutating like crazy in all that filth. And they keep trying to get through with infiltrators to give *us* the latest strain, don't they?

The Chinese and the Iranians, they *kill* their black-carders, don't they? The Japs, they deport them to Korea. And the Russians, they nuked themselves a cordon sanitaire all the way from the Caspian to the Chinese border.

Was I old Walter T., I'd say nuke the whole cesspit of

5

infection out of existence. Use nerve gas. Fry the Third World clean from orbit. Whatever. They gave us the damn Plague, didn't they? Way we see it in the Army of the Living Dead, anything we do after that is only a little piece of what the gorks got coming!

Believe me, this poor boy wasn't shedding any tears for what we had done to the Mexes when the marks starting coming out just before the sack of Ensenada. Less still when they couldn't come up with a combo of pallies that worked anymore, and they shrugged and finally told me it looked like I had reached Condition Terminal in the ruins of La Paz. Like I said, when I first Got It, they gave me six years, ten in the Army of the Living Dead.

Now they gave me six months.

I shot up with about a hundred milligrams of liquid crystal, chugalugged a quart of tequila, and butt-fucked every gork I could find. Think I blew about ten of them away afterward, but by then, brothers and sisters, who the hell was counting?

WALTER T. BIGELOW

OH YES, I KNOW WHAT THEY SAY ABOUT ME BEHIND MY BACK, EVEN on a cabinet level. Old Walter T., he was a virgin when he married Elaine, and he's never even had meat with his own pure Christian wife. Old Walter T., he's never even stuck it in a sex machine. Old Walter T., he's never even missed the pleasures of the flesh. Old Walter T., he'd still be the same sexless eunuch even if there had never been a Plague. Old Walter T., he's got holy water for blood.

How little they know of my torments.

How little they know of what it was like for me in high school. In the locker room. With all those naked male bodies. All the little tricks I had to learn to hide my erections. Knowing what I was. Knowing it was a sin. Unable to look my own father squarely in the eye.

Walter Bigelow found Christ at the age of seventeen and was Born Again, that's what the official biography says. Alas, it was only partly true. Oh yes, I dedicated my life to Jesus when I was seventeen. But it was a cold, logical decision. It seemed the only means of controlling my unwholesome urges, the only way I could avoid damnation.

I hated God then. I hated Him for making me what I was and condemning me to hellfire should I succumb to the temptations of my own God-given nature. I believed in God, but I hated Him. I believed in Jesus, but how could I believe that Jesus believed in me?

I was not granted Grace until I was twenty.

My college roommate Gus was a torment. He flaunted his naked body in what seemed like total innocence. He masturbated under the bedclothes at night while I longed to be there with him.

One morning he walked into the bathroom while I was toweling myself down after a shower. He was nude, with an enormous erection. I could not keep my flesh from responding in kind. He confessed his lust for me. I let him touch me. I found myself reaching for his manhood.

He offered to do anything. My powers of resistance were at a low point. We indulged in mutual masturbation. I would go no further.

For months we engaged in this onanistic act, Gus offering me every fleshly delight I had ever fantasized, I calling on Christ to save me.

Finally, a moment came when I could resist no longer. Gus knelt on the floor before me, running his hands over my body, cupping my buttocks. I was lost. His mouth reached out for me—

And at that moment God at last granted me His Grace.

As his head lowered, I saw the Devil's mark upon the

back of his neck, small as yet, but unmistakable—Kaposi's sarcoma.

Gus had the Plague.

He was about to give it to me.

I leaped backward. Gus was an instrument of the Devil sent to damn my flesh to the Plague and my soul to everlasting torment.

And at last I understood. I saw that it was *the Devil,* not God, who had tormented me with these unwholesome urges. And God had let me suffer them as a test and a preparation. A test of my worthiness and a preparation for this moment of revelation of His Divine Mercy. For had He not chosen to show me the Sign that saved me from my own sinful nature at this eleventh hour?

That was when I was granted true Grace.

I sank to my knees and gave thanks to God. *That* was when I was Born Again. *That* was when I became a true Christian. That too was when I was shown my true calling, when the vision opened up before me.

God had allowed the Devil to inflict the Plague on man to test us, even as I had been tested, for to succumb to the temptations of the flesh was to succumb to the Plague and be dragged, rotting and screaming, to Hell.

This was the fate that Jesus had saved me from, for only the Sign He had shown me had preserved me from death and eternal damnation. My life, therefore, was truly His, and what I must use it for was to protect mankind from this Plague and its carriers, to save those I could as Jesus had saved me.

And He spoke to me in my heart. "Become a leader of

men," Jesus told me. "Save them from themselves. Do My work in the world."

I promised Him that I would. I would do it in the only way I could conceive of, through politics.

I became a prelaw major. I entered law school. I graduated with honors. I found, courted, and married a pure Christian virgin, and soon thereafter impregnated Elaine with Billy, ran for the Virginia State Assembly, and was elected.

The rest of my life is, as they say, history.

LINDA LEWIN

I WAS JUST ANOTHER HORNY SPOILED LITTLE BRAT UNTIL I GOT IT, just like all my horny spoiled little friends in Berkeley. Upper-middle-class family with an upper-middle-class house in the hills. My own car for my sixteenth birthday, along with the latest model sex interface.

Oh yes, they did! My mom and dad were no Unholy Rollers, they were educated intellectual liberal Democrats, they read all the literature, they had been children of the Sexy Seventies, they were realists, they knew the score.

These are terrible times, they told me. We know you'll be tempted to have meat. You might get away with it for years. Or you might Get It the first time out. Don't risk it, Linda. We know how you feel, we remember when everyone did meat. We know this is unnatural. But we know the consequences, and so do you.

And they dragged me out on the porch and made me look out across the Bay at San Francisco. The Bay Bridge with its blown-out center span. The pig boats patrolling the shore-line. The gunships buzzing about the periphery like angry horseflies.

Meat City. That's where you'd end up, Linda. Nothing's worth that, now is it?

I nodded. But even then, I wondered.

I had grown up with the vision of the shining city across the Bay. Oh yes, I had also grown up knowing that the lovely hills and graceful buildings and sparkling night lights masked a charnel house of the Plague, black-carders all, 100 percent. We were told horror stories about it in sex hygiene classes starting in kindergarten.

But from about the fifth grade on, we told ourselves our own stories too. We whispered them in the ladies' room. We uploaded them onto bulletin boards. We downloaded them, printed them out, wiped them from memory so our parents wouldn't see them, masturbated over the printouts.

As porn went, it was crude, amateurish stuff. What could you expect from teenage virgins? And it was all the same. A teenager Gets It. And runs away to San Francisco. Or disappears into the underground. And, sentenced to death already, sets out to enjoy all the pleasures of the meat on the way out, in crude, lurid, sensational detail. And of course, the porn sheets all ended long before Condition Terminal was reached.

But I was a good little girl and I was a smart little girl and the sex interface my parents gave me was the best money could buy, not some cheap one-way hooker's model. It had everything. The vaginal insert was certified to five atmospheres, but it was only fifty microns thick, heated to blood temperature, and totally flexible. It had a neat little clithood programmed for five varieties of electric stimulation and six vibratory patterns. I could wear the thing under my jeans, finger the controls, and never fail to come, even in the dullest math class.

The guys said that the interior lining was the max, tight and soft and wet, the stim programs the best there were. But what did they know? Who among them had ever felt real meat?

Oh yes, it was a wonderful sex interface my parents gave me to protect me from the temptations of the meat.

And of course I hated the damned thing.

Worse still when the guy I was balling with it insisted on wearing *his* interface too. Yech! His penile sheath in my vaginal insert. Like two sex machines doing it to each other. I remember an awful thing I did to one wimp who really pissed me off. I took off my interface, made him take off his, inserted his penile sheath in my vaginal insert, activated both interfaces, and made him sit there with me watching the two things go at each other without us for a solid hour.

And then there came Rex.

What can I say about Rex? I was eighteen. He was a year younger. He was beautiful. We never made it through two interfaces. I'd wear mine or he'd wear his and we'd go at it for hours. It was wonderful. We swore eternal love. We took to telling each other meatporn stories as we did it. This was it, I knew it was, we were soul mates for life. Rex swore up and down that he had never done meat and so did I. So why not . . .

Finally we did.

We took off our interfaces and did meat together. We tried out everything in those meatporn stories and then

13

some. Every orifice. Every variation. Every day for two months.

Well, to make the usual long sad story short and nasty, I had been telling the truth, but Rex hadn't. And I had to learn about it from my parents.

Your boyfriend Rex's Got It, they told me one bright sunny morning. He's been black-carded and they've dropped him in San Francisco. You and he never . . . you didn't . . . because if you did, we're going to have to turn you in, you know that, don't you?

Well, of course I freaked. But it was a cold slow-motion freak, with everything running through my head too fast for me to panic. I had a whole month till my next ID exam. I knew damn well my card would come up black. What should I do? Let them drop me in San Francisco and go out in a blaze of meatfucking glory with Rex? Yeah, sure, with the lying son of a bitch who had killed me!

I thought fast. I lied up and down. I threw an outraged temper tantrum when my parents suggested maybe I should go in for an early check. I convinced them. Or maybe I just let them convince themselves.

I found myself an underground doc and checked myself out. Got It. I drifted into the Berkeley underground, not as difficult as you might think for a girl who was willing to give meat to the secret Living Dead for a few dollars and a few more connections. I learned about how they kept ahead of the Sex Police. I learned about the phony blue cards. And I made my plans.

When I had hooked enough to score one, I got myself a primo counterfeit. As long as I found myself a wizard every three months to update the data strip, it would show blue.

I could stay free until I died, unless of course I got picked up by the SP and got my card run against the national data bank, in which case I would turn up null and it would all be over.

I hooked like crazy, three, four, five tricks a day. I piled up a bankroll and kept it in bills. The day before I was to report for my ID update, I got in my car to go to school, said the usual goodbye to my parents, and took off, headed south.

South to Santa Cruz. South to L.A. South to anywhere. Out along the broad highway to see what there was to see of California, of what was left of America, out along the broad highway toward the eventual inevitable—crazed, confused, terror-stricken, brave with fatal knowledge, determined only to have a long hot run till my time ran out.

DR. RICHARD BRUNO

THEY USED TO CALL IT MIDLIFE CRISIS, MALE MENOPAUSE, THE seven-year itch, back when it wasn't a condition to which you were condemned for life at birth.

I was just about to turn forty. I had dim teenage memories of quite a meaty little sex life back at the beginning of the Ugly Eighties, before the Plague, before I married Marge. Oh yes, I had been quite a hot little cocksman before it all fell apart, a child of the last half-generation of the Sexual Revolution.

When I was Tod's age, fifteen, I had already had more real meat than the poor frustrated little guy was likely to get in his whole life. Now I had to watch my own son sneaking around to sleazy sex parlors to stick it into sex machines, and don't think I was above it myself from time to time.

Marge, well . . .

Marge was five years younger than I. Just young enough

to never have known what the real thing was like, young enough to remember nothing but condoms and vaginal dams and the early interfaces. Oh yes, we had meat together in the early years, before it finally resulted in Tod. Poor Marge was terrified the whole time, unable to come. After Tod was born, she got herself an interface, and never made love again without it.

Marge still loved me, I think, and I still loved her, but the Plague Years had dried her up sexually, turned her prudish and sour. She wouldn't even let me buy Tod an interface so he could get it from a real girl, if only secondhand. His sixteenth birthday is more than time enough, she insisted shrilly every time we fought about it, which was frequently.

Naturally, or perhaps more accurately unnaturally, all my libidinal energies had long since been channeled into my work. It was the perfect sublimation.

I was a genetic synthesizer for the Sutcliffe Corporation in Palo Alto. I had already designed five different Plague vaccines for Sutcliffe that made them hundreds of millions each before the virus mutated into immunity. I was the fair-haired boy. I got many bonuses. I had my own private lab with little restraint on my budget. For a scientist, it should have been heaven.

It wasn't.

It was maddening. A new Plague strain would appear and rise to dominance. I'd strip off the antigen coat, clone it, insert its genome in a bacterium, and Sutcliffe would market a vaccine to those who could afford it, make hundreds of millions in six months. Then the next immune strain would appear, and it would be back to square one. I felt like a scientific Sisyphus, rolling the dead weight of the Plague uphill, only to have it roll back and crush my hopes every six months.

Was I taking my work a bit too personally? Of course I was. My "personal life" consisted of the occasional interface sex with Marge, which I had long since come to loathe, watching my son sneaking around to sex machine parlors, and the occasional trip there myself. My "personal life" had been stolen from me by the Plague, by the Enemy, so of course I took my work personally.

I was obsessed. My work *was* my personal life. And I had a vision.

Cassette vaccines had been around for decades. Strip down a benign virus, plug in sets of antigens off several target organisms, and hey, presto, antibodies to several diseases conferred in a single shot.

Why not apply the same technique to the Plague? Strip one strain down to the core, hang it with antigen coats from four or five strains at once, and confer multistrain immunity. Certainly not to every mutation, but if I could develop an algorithm that could predict mutations, if I could develop cassette vaccines that *stayed ahead* of the viral mutations, might I not somehow be able eventually to force the Plague to mutate out?

Oh yes, I took the battle personally, or so I admitted to myself at the time. Little did I know just how personal it was about to become.

JOHN DAVID

No SOONER HAD WE FINISHED MOPPING UP IN LA PAZ THAN MY UNIT was airlifted up to the former Mexican border as part of the force that would keep it sealed until the SPs could set up their cordon. Through the luck of the draw, we got the sweetest billet, holding the line between Tijuana and San Diego.

They kept us zombies south of the former border, you better believe they didn't want us in Dago, no way they would let us set foot on real American soil, but meatfucker, you wouldn't *believe* the scene in TJ!

Back before the Plague, the place had been one big whore-house and drug supermarket anyway. For fifteen years it had been a haven for underground black-carders, Latino would-be infiltrators, black pally docs, dealers in every contraband item that existed, getting poorer and more desperate as the cordon around Mexico tightened.

Now TJ found itself in the process of becoming an American Quarantine Zone, and it was Bugfuck City. Mexicans trying to get into Dago on false passports and blue cards. Wanted Americans trying to get out to anywhere. False IDs going for outrageous prices. Pussy and ass and drugs and uncertified pharmaceuticals and armaments going for whatever the poor bastards left holding them could get.

And the law, such as it was, until the SPs could replace the Legion, was *us,* brothers and sisters. Unbelievable! We could buy anything—drugs, phony blue cards, six-year-old virgins, you name it—or just have what we wanted at gunpoint. And money hand over fist, I mean we looted everything with no law but us to stop us, and did heavy traffic in government arms on top of it.

Loaded with money, we stayed stoned and drunk and turned that town into our twenty-four-hour pigpen, you better believe it! No one more so than me, brothers and sisters, with those marks coming out, knowing this could be my last big night to party.

I scored half a dozen phony blue cards and corroborating papers to match. I stuffed my pockets with money. I shot up with every half-baked pally TJ had to peddle, and they had everything from Russian biologicals to ground-up nun's tits in holy water. If this was my Condition Terminal, I was determined to take as much of the world with me as I could before I went out. I meatfucked myself deaf, dumb, and blind and must've Given It to five hundred Mexes in the bargain.

Then they started phasing in the Sex Police. Well, as you might imagine, there was no love lost between the Army of the Living Dead and the SPs. Those uptight Unholy Rollers took any opportunity to snuff us. Looters were shot. Meatfuckers caught in the act were executed. And of course, brothers and sisters, the Army of the Living Dead gave as good as we got and then some.

We'd kill any of the bastards we caught on what remained of our shrinking turf. We'd get up kamikaze packs and go into their turf after them. When we were really loaded, we'd catch ourselves some SP assholes and gang-bang them senseless. Needless to say, we weren't into using interfaces.

Things got so out of hand that the Pentagon brought in regular airborne troops to round us up. That little action took more casualties in two days than the whole Baja campaign had in three weeks.

When they started dropping napalm from close-support fighters, it finally dawned on those of us still around that the meatfuckers had no intention of rounding us up and shipping us to the next theater. They were out to kill us all, and they were probably working themselves up to tactical nukes to do it.

Well, we weren't the Army of the Living Dead for nothing. I don't know where it started or who started it. It just seemed to happen all at once. Somehow all of us that were left stuffed our loot in our packs, armed ourselves with whatever we could lay hands on, and suddenly there was a human wave assault on the border.

It was the bloodiest ragged combat any of us ever saw, crazed zombies against gunships, fighters, and tanks. How many of the bastards did we get on the way? More than you might imagine, better believe it, we were stoned, drunk, in a berserker rage, and we were now the Living Dead twice over, with Double Nothing to lose, triple so for yours truly.

How many of us got through? A thousand? Five hundred?

Something to keep you from oversleeping, citizens. Hundreds of us zombies, our packs stuffed with money, false IDs, and ordnance, over the border into San Diego, hunted, dying, betrayed by even the Army, with nothing left for kicks but to take our vengeance on *you*, meatfuckers!

And I was one of them. The meanest and the craziest, it pleases me to believe. Betrayed, facing Condition Terminal, with nothing left to do with what little was left of my life but bop till I dropped and take as many of you as I could with me.

LINDA LEWIN

I DROVE AIMLESSLY AROUND CALIFORNIA FOR MONTHS, DOWN 101 or the Coast Highway to Los Angeles, down 5 to San Diego, up to L.A. again, up 5 to the Bay Area, back around again, like a squirrel in a cage, like one of those circuit-riding preachers in an old Western.

I Had It. My days were numbered. I needed cash—for gas, for food, for a flop in a motel, for what pallies I could score, for updating the data strip on my phony blue card. I hooked wherever I could, using my interface always, for I swore to myself that I would never do to anyone what Rex had done to me. I didn't want to go to Condition Terminal with *that* mark on my soul.

Bit by bit, inch by inch, I drifted into the underground. You'd be surprised how many black-carders there were surviving outside the Quarantine Zones on phony IDs, a secret America within America, hiding within plain sight of the SPs, living by our wits and our own code.

We found one another by some kind of second sight impossible to explain. Pally pushers. ID wizards. Hookers just like me.

And not like me.

There were bars where we met to trade in pallies and IDs and information. You met all kinds. Pally dealers and drug dealers. ID wizards. Hookers like me, male and female, selling interface sex to the solid citizens. And hookers of the other kind.

Hookers selling meat.

It was amazing how many blue-carders were willing to risk death for the real thing. It was amazing how innocent some of them were willing to be. At first I refused to believe the stories the meatwhores told in the bars, cackling evilly all the time. I refused to believe that they were knowingly spreading the Plague and laughing about it. I refused to believe that blue-carders could be so stupid.

But they were and they could. And after a while, I understood.

There were people who would pay fantastic prices for meatsex with another certified blue-carder. There were clandestine meatbars where they hung out, bars with ID readers. Pick up one of these fools, pop your phony card in a reader, and watch their eyes light up as the strip read out blue, no line to the national data banks here, not with the SPs raiding any such bar they could get a line on. And you got paid more for a quick meatfuck than you could earn in a week of interface hooking.

Sure I was tempted. There was more to it than the money. Didn't I long for meat myself? Wasn't that how I had Gotten

24

It in the first place? Didn't these damn blue-card assholes deserve what they got?

Who knows, I might have ended up doing it in the end if I hadn't met Saint Max, Our Lady of the Flowers.

Saint Max was a black-carder. He carried his own ID reader around and he didn't worry about phony cards reading out blue.

Saint Max would give meat only to certified *black*-carders, and he would never refuse anyone, even the most rotted-out Terminals.

I was in an underground bar in Santa Monica when Saint Max walked in, and half a dozen people told me his story before I ever heard it from his lips. Saint Max was a legend of the California underground. The only real hero we had.

Max was a bisexual, male or female, it didn't matter to him, and he never took money. People fed him, bought him drinks, gave him the latest pallies, found him free flop, sent him on his way. "I am dependent on the kindness of strangers," Max used to say. And in return, any black-carder stranger could depend on kindness from him.

Max was old; in terms of how long he had survived with God knew how many Plague strains inside him, he was ancient. He had lived in the San Francisco Quarantine Zone before it was a Quarantine Zone. And he was a man with a mission. He had this crazy theory.

I heard it from him that night after I had bought him a meal and about half a dozen drinks.

"I'm a living reservoir of every Plague strain extant, my dear," he told me. "And I do my best to keep up with the latest mutations."

25

Max believed that all black-carders had a moral obligation to have as much meatsex with one another as possible. So as to speed the pace of evolution. In a large enough pool of cross-infected Plague victims the virus might mutate out into something benign. Or a multiimmunity might evolve and spread quickly. A pathogen that killed its host was, after all, a maladapted organism, and as long as it was killing us, so were we.

"Natural selection, my dear. In the long run, it's our species' only hope. In the long run, everyone is going to Get It, and it's going to get most of us. But if out of the billions who will die, evolution eventually selects for multiimmunity, or a benign Plague variant, the human race will survive. And for as long as all these pallies keep me going, I intend to serve the process."

It seemed crazy to me, and I told him so, exposing yourself to every Plague strain you could. Didn't that mean Condition Terminal would just come quicker?

Saint Max shrugged. "Here I am," he said. "No one's been exposed to as many Plague variants as me. Maybe it's already happened. Maybe I've got multiimmunity. Maybe I'm a mutant. Maybe there's already a benign strain inside me."

He smiled sadly. "We're all under sentence of death the moment we're born anyway, now aren't we, my dear? Even the poor blue-carders. It's only a matter of how, and when, and in the pursuit of what. And like old John Henry, I intend to die with my hammer in my hand. Think about it, Linda."

And I did. I offered Max a ride up the coast and he accepted and we ended up traveling one full slow cycle of my circuit together. I watched Max giving meat freely to one and all, to kids like me new to the underground, to thieves, and whores, and horrible Terminals on the way out. No one took Saint Max's crazy theory seriously. Everyone loved him.

And so did I. I paid my way with the usual interface sex, and Max let it be until we were finally back in Santa Monica and it was time to say goodbye. "You're young, Linda," he told me. "With good enough pallies, you have years ahead of you. Me, I know I'm reaching the end of the line. You've got the heart for it, my dear. This old faggot would go out a lot happier knowing that there was someone like you to carry on. Think about it, my dear, 'A Short Life but a Happy One,' as they say in the Army of the Living Dead. And don't think we're not all in it."

I thought about it. I thought about it for a long time. But I didn't do anything about it till I saw Max again, till Max lay dying.

WALTER T. BIGELOW

AFTER TWO TERMS IN THE VIRGINIA ASSEMBLY, I RAN FOR CONGRESS and was elected. Capitol Hill was in a state of uproar over the Plague. National policy was nonexistent. Some states were quarantining Plague victims, others were doing nothing. Some states were testing people at their borders, others were calling this a violation of the Constitution. Some representatives were calling for a national health identity card, others considered this a civil rights outrage. Christian groups were calling for a national quarantine policy. Plague victims' rights groups were calling for an end to all restrictions on their free movements. Dozens of test cases were moving ponderously toward the Supreme Court.

After two terms watching this congressional paralysis, God inspired me to conceive of the National Quarantine Amendment. I ran for the Senate on it, received the support of Christians and Plague victims alike, and was elected by a huge majority.

The amendment nationalized Plague policy. Each state was required to set up Quarantine Zones proportional in area and economic base to the percentage of victims in its territory, said division to be updated every two years. Every citizen outside a Zone must carry an updated blue card. In return for this, Plague victims were guaranteed full civil and voting rights within their Quarantine Zones, and free commerce in nonbiological products was assured.

It was fair. It was just. It was inspired by God. Under my leadership it sailed through Congress and was accepted by three-quarters of the states within two years after I led a strenuous nationwide campaign to pass it.

I was a national hero. It was a presidential year. I was told that I was assured my party's nomination, that my election to the presidency was all but certain.

LINDA LEWIN

Saint Max had suddenly collapsed into late Condition Terminal. Indeed he was at the point of death when I finally followed the trail of the sad story to a cabin on a seacliff not far from Big Sur. There he lay, skeletal, emaciated, his body covered with sarcomas, semicomatose.

But his eyes opened up when I walked in. "I've been waiting for you, my dear," he said. "I wasn't about to leave without saying goodbye to Our Lady."

"Our Lady? That's *you,* Max."

"*Was,* my dear."

"Oh, Max . . ." I cried, and burst into tears. "What can I do?"

"Nothing, my dear . . . Or everything." His eyes were hard and pitiless then, yet also somehow soft and imploring.

"Max . . ."

He nodded. "You could give me one last meatfuck goodbye," he told me. He smiled. "I would have preferred a boy, of course, but at least it would please my old mother to know that I mended my ways on my deathbed."

I looked at his feverish, disease-ravaged body. "You don't know what you're asking!" I cried.

"Oh yes I do, my dear. I'm asking you to do the bravest thing you've ever done in your life. I'm asking you to believe in the faith of a dying madman. On the other hand, I'm asking for nothing at all, since you've already Got It."

How could I not? Either way, he was right. The Plague would kill me sooner or later no matter what I did now. I would never even know by how much this act of kindness would shorten my life span. Or if it would at all. And Max was dying. He had lived his life bravely in the service of humanity, at least as he saw it. And I loved him more in that moment than I had ever loved anyone in my life. And what if he was right? What other hope did humanity have? How could I refuse him?

I couldn't.

I didn't.

Afterward, as I held him, he spoke to me one last time. "Now for my last wish," he said.

"Haven't I just given it to you?"

"You know you haven't."

"What then?"

"You know, my dear."

So I did. I had accepted it when I took his ravaged manhood inside my unprotected body. I knew that now. I knew that I had known it all along.

"Will you take up this torch from me?" he said, holding out his hand.

31

"Yes, Max, I will," I promised and reached for the phantom object.

"Then this old faggot can go out happy," he said. And died in my arms with a smile on his lips.

And I became Our Lady. Our Lady of the Living Dead, as they were to call me.

JOHN DAVID

SAN DIEGO WAS CRAWLING WITH SPS, AND THEY PROBABLY WOULD
have sent in commando units to hunt us down, if they
weren't so terrified of what would happen if the citizens were
to find out that hundreds of us zombies were loose and on
the warpath in the good old U.S. of A.

And we were, meatfuckers, better believe it! Wouldn't
you? Sooner or later they were going to get us all, and if
they didn't, the Plague would, and in my case, sooner than
later. So we scattered. I don't know what the others did, but
me, I stayed drunk and stoned, and meatfucked as many of
the treacherous blue-carders as I could lay my hands on. And
tracked down all the pally pushers I could find. I don't even
know what half the stuff I shot up was, but something in
the mix, or maybe the mix itself, seemed to slow the Plague.
I didn't get any better, but I seemed to stabilize.

But the situation in Dago didn't, brothers and sisters. It
became one close call after another. Finally I got caught by

a couple of stupid SPs. Well, those Unholy Rollers were no match for a zombie with my combat smarts. While they were running one of my phony cards through the national data bank and coming up null, I managed to kill the meatfuckers.

I picked my IDs off the corpses, but now the national data bank had me marked as a zombie on the run, and when they found these stiffs, they'd fax my photo to every SP station in the fifty states. The Sex Police took a real dim view of SP killers, and nailing me would be priority one.

I had only one chance, not that it was max probability. I had to disappear into a Quarantine Zone. San Francisco was the biggest, hence the safest. Also the tastiest, or so I was told.

So I snatched a car and headed north. How I would break *into* a Zone, I'd have to figure out later. If, by some chance, I managed to avoid the SPs long enough to get there.

WALTER T. BIGELOW

CONGRESS SET UP THE FEDERAL QUARANTINE AGENCY TO ADMINIS-
ter the National Quarantine Amendment. It would have
enormous power and enormous responsibility. It was the
wisdom of Congress, with which I heartily concurred, that
it be entirely insulated from party politics. The director
would be chosen in the manner of Supreme Court justices—
nominated by the president, approved by the Senate, serving
for life, removable only by impeachment.

After the president signed the bill, he called me into his
office and pleaded with me to accept the appointment. It
was my amendment. I was the only political figure who had
the confidence of both Plague victims and blue-carders.

All that, I knew, was true. What was also true was that
many insiders blanched at the thought of a Bigelow presidency. This was the perfect political solution.

It was the most important decision of my life and the
most difficult. Elaine had had her heart set on being First

Lady. "You just *can't* let them take the presidency away from you like this," she insisted. Ministers and black-carder groups and politicians of my own party, some sincere, some otherwise, begged me to accept the lifetime directorship of the FQA. For weeks, they all badgered me while I procrastinated and prayed.

It seemed as if the voices of God and the Devil were speaking to me through my wife, party leaders, men of God, men of power, saints and sinners, battling for possession of my soul. But which was the voice of God and which the voice of Satan? Which way did my true duty lie? What did God want me to do?

Finally, I went on a solitary retreat into the Utah desert, into Zion National Park. I fasted. I prayed. I called on Jesus to speak to me.

And at length a voice did speak to me, in a vision. "You are the Moses I have chosen to lead My people out of the wilderness," it told me. "Have I not commanded you to become a leader of men? Those who would deny you power are the agents of the Adversary."

But then another stronger and sweeter voice spoke out of a great white light and I knew that this was truly Jesus and whose the first voice had really been.

"I saved you from the Plague and your own sinful desire in your hour of need," He told me. "I raised you up from the pit so that you might do God's will on Earth. As I gave up My life to save Man from sin, so must you give up worldly power to save the people from their dark natures. As God chose Me for My Calvary, so do I choose you for yours."

I returned from the desert to Washington and I obeyed. I put the thought of worldly glory behind me. There were those who snickered when I accepted this appointment. There were those who laughed when I told the nation that I had done it at the bidding of Jesus.

Even my wife told me I was a fool, and a breach was opened between us that I knew no way to heal. We became strangers to each other sharing the same marriage bed.

Oh yes, I paid dearly for my obedience to God's will. But while I may have lost my chance at worldly power and hardened my wife's heart against me, I remained steadfast and strong.

For God had saved me in that dormitory room with Gus and granted me Grace and salvation. And Jesus spoke truth to me in the desert in the presence of the Adversary and saved me again. And so in my heart I knew I had done right.

DR. RICHARD BRUNO

How could I have done such a thing? How could I, of all people, have been naïve enough to Get It from a meatwhore? As the ancient saying has it, a stiff dick knows no conscience, and they don't call a fool a stupid prick for nothing.

For my fortieth birthday, I got royally drunk and righteously stoned, and I demanded a special birthday present from Marge. Was it really too much to ask from one's own wife on the night of the rite de passage of my midlife crisis? Tender loving meat for my Fateful Fortieth? We were both blue-carders. Marge had hardly any sex life at all. The only times I had been unfaithful to her were with radiation-sterilized sex machines.

I was loaded and raving, but she was entirely irrational. She refused. When I attempted to get physical, she locked herself in the bedroom and told me to go stick it in one of my goddamn sex machines.

I reeled out into the streets, stoned out of my mind, aching with despair, with a raging fortieth-birthday hard-on. But I didn't slink off to the usual sex machine parlor, oh no; that was what Marge had told me to do, wasn't it?

Instead, I found myself one of those clandestine meatbars. To make the old long story modern and short, I picked up a whore. We inserted our cards in the bar's reader and of course they both came up blue. Off I went to her room and did every kind of meat I could think of and some that seemed to be her own inventions.

I staggered home, still loaded, and passed out on the couch. The Morning After . . .

Oh my God!

Beyond the inevitable horrid hangover and conjugal re-criminations, I awoke to the full awfulness of what I had done. In my present sober and thoroughly detumescent state, I knew all too well how many phony blue cards were floating around the meatbars. Had I . . . ?

I ran the standard tests on myself in my own lab for six days. On the sixth day, they came up black. When I cultured the bastard, it turned out to be a Plague variant I had not yet seen.

By this time I had prepared myself for the inevitable. I had made my plans. As fortune would have it, I had ten weeks before my next ID update, ten weeks to achieve what medical science had failed to achieve in twenty years and more of trying.

But I had motivation. If I failed, in ten weeks I would lose my blue card, my job, my mission in life, my wife, my family, and with no one to blame but myself. At this point, I wasn't even thinking about the fact that I was under sentence of eventual death. What would happen in ten weeks was more than disaster enough to keep me working twenty hours a day, or so at least it seemed.

And, crazed creature that I was, I had a crazy idea, one that, in retrospect, I saw I had been moving toward all along.

My work on cassette vaccines was already well advanced, so might it not be possible to push it one step further, and synthesize an *automatic self-programming* cassette vaccine? It might be pushing the edge of the scientific possible, but it was my only hope. A crazy idea, yes, but was not madness just over the edge from inspiration?

I stripped a Plague virus down to the harmless core in the usual manner. But I didn't start hanging on the usual series of antigen coat variants. I started crafting a series of nano-manipulators out of RNA fragments, molecular "tentacles."

What I was after was an organism that would infect the same cells as the Plague. That would seize any strain of Plague virus it found, destroy the core, and wrap the empty antigen coat around itself, much as a hermit crab crawls inside a discarded seashell in order to protect its nakedness from the world.

In effect, a killed-virus vaccine that could still reproduce as an organism, an organism continually reprogramming its antigen coat to mimic lethal invaders, that would use the corpses of the Enemy to stimulate the production of anti-bodies to it, a living, self-programming cassette vaccine factory within my own body.

The theory was simple, cunning, and elegant. Actually synthesizing such a molecular dreadnaught was something else again . . .

LINDA LEWIN

THE STORY OF WHAT HAPPENED ON SAINT MAX'S DEATHBED BECAME a legend of the underground. And whereas Max had been old and had long since outlived any rational expectations of survival, I was young, I appeared healthy, and so what I was risking was readily apparent.

Like Saint Max, Our Lady gave the comfort of her meat to anyone who asked her. I gave freely of my body to young black-carders like myself, to rotting Terminals, to every underground black-carder between.

Perhaps because I was young, perhaps because I was the first convert to Saint Max's vision daring enough to put it into practice, perhaps because I was so much more naïvely earnest about it than he had been, perhaps because I appeared to be in such robust health, there were those who believed in it now, who believed in me, in the Faith of Our Lady. If Saint Max had been our Jesus, and I was our Paul, now there

41

were disciples to spread the Faith, no more than scores, maybe, but at least more than Christianity's original twelve.

Spreading the Faith of Saint Max and Our Lady. Gaining converts with our hope and our bodies as we wandered up and down California. The Plague strains would spread faster now. Millions might die sooner who might have lingered longer. But were we not all under sentence of death anyway, blue-carders and black-carders alike?

Millions of lives might be shortened, but out of all that death, the species might survive. We would challenge the Plague head-on, in the only way we could—love against despair, sex against death. We would force the pace of evolution and/or die trying.

And while we lived, we would at least live free, we would live, and love, and fight for our species' survival as natural men and women. Better in fire than in ice.

WALTER T. BIGELOW

I HAD DONE AS GOD COMMANDED, I WAS DOING HIS WORK, BUT THE Devil continued to torment me. Elaine remained distant and cold, the Plague continued to spread despite my best efforts, and then, at length, Satan, not content with this, reached out and put his hand upon my Billy.

Billy, the son I had raised so carefully, the son who to my joy had Found the Light at the age of fourteen, began to act strangely, moping in his room at night, locking himself in the bathroom for suspiciously long intervals. I didn't need to be the director of the Federal Quarantine Agency to suspect what was happening; any good Christian father could read the signs.

I was prepared to find pornography when I searched his room one morning after he had left for school, but nothing could have prepared me for the vile nature of the filth I found. Photographs of men having meatsex with each other. With young boys. Photographs of naked young boys in the lewdest of poses. And, worse still, hideous cartoons of boys and girls having the most impossible and revolting intercourse with sex machines, automated monstrosities with grotesque vulvas, immense penile organs, done up to simulate animals, robots, tentacled aliens from outer space.

I reeled. My skin crawled. My stomach went cold. Worst of all, the Devil caused my weak flesh to become loathsomely aroused as all those terrible and tantalizing memories of Gus came rushing back between my legs to haunt me.

Revolted, appalled, shaking with outrage and confusion, I was forced to wait until the evening to confront him, and the Devil struck me a second blow in the office, for that was the day when the first reports of the Satanic cult of Our Lady of the Living Dead appeared in my electronic mailbox.

Of course I was aware that there were hundreds of thousands, perhaps millions, of black-carders living underground outside the Quarantine Zones on bogus blue cards, and spreading their filth among the innocent. We caught hundreds of them every week.

But this . . . this . . . this was Satan's masterstroke!

Out there in California was a woman, or perhaps several women, known as Our Lady of the Living Dead, clearly possessed by the Adversary and doing his work quite consciously, recruiting others into her Satanic cult, spreading his lies and the Plague in ever-wider circles.

Black-carders were openly offering their meat to their fellow black-carders, spreading multiple strains of Plague virus throughout the underground. Interrogations seemed to indicate that these slaves of Satan actually believed that they were the saviors of the species, that in some mystical manner they were speeding the course of evolution, that somehow out of their unholy and deadly couplings a strain of humanity would evolve that was immune to the Plague.

He is not the Prince of Liars for nothing. He had apparently quite convinced these poor doomed creatures of this one, cunningly using their despair-maddened lust and turning it against us all, giving them a truly devilish excuse to wallow in it until they died in the conviction that they were doing God's Work in the process.

And laughing at them and at me by causing his servant to wrap herself in the cognomen of the Mother of Jesus!

I gave the necessary orders. The stamping out of the cult of Our Lady was to be the SP's number one priority. Arrest these people. If any resisted, shoot to kill. Close as many meatbars as possible. And do it all as conspicuously as could be managed. Spread the fear of God's wrath and that of the SP among the denizens of the underground.

After a day like that, I was constrained to return home and confront Billy. There was denial, sobbing confession, promises of repentance, and strong penances set. I had done my patriotic duty and my fatherly duty. It had been hard, but I had done God's will and was as much at peace as one could be under the terrible circumstances.

But Satan was still not finished with me. He seized Elaine, my good Christian wife, and caused her to launch into the most appalling tirade. "How can you be so hard-hearted?" she demanded. "Aren't things bad enough for young people growing up these days? At least you shouldn't try to keep Billy from a little safe masturbation."

"It's against God's law! Besides, you saw that revolting, unnatural—"

"Of course it's unnatural, Walter! What else can you expect when the most natural thing in the world is the one thing none of us can do anymore!"

"Elaine—"

"If you were a real man, Walter T. Bigelow, if you were a real Christian, if you were a real loving father, you'd take the poor boy to a sex machine parlor and show him how to get some harmless release!"

I could hardly believe my ears for a long moment. This could not be Elaine! But then I understood. This insinuating blasphemy was coming from her lips, but my poor wife was only an instrument. The voice saying these awful things through her had identified itself by the very act of causing a good Christian woman to mouth them.

"I know you . . ." I muttered.

"No you don't, Walter Bigelow, you don't know me at all!"

"Get thee behind me—"

"Have it your own way!" she shouted. And she locked herself in the bedroom, leaving me to spend a sleepless night in the living room, praying to Jesus, demanding to know why He had so forsaken me in the presence of the Enemy.

JOHN DAVID

I MADE MY WAY UP THE COAST TOWARD SAN FRANCISCO REAL SLOW-
ly, spending nearly a month in Los Angeles, which was big,
and sprawling, and a hell of a town for a zombie to party in.
There were plenty of meatbars, my latest batch of pallies
seemed to be holding up real well, I was lookin' good, I had
umpteen phony blue cards, and I was able to meatfuck myself near to exhaustion. It was almost too easy.

And then one night I found out why.

I let myself get picked up on the street by this sexy space
case who told me she'd give me free meat if I was a *black*-
carder, if you can believe that one. Well, she was beautiful,
I was real stoned and in a kind of funny mood, so I shoved
her into an alley, Gave It to her, and then announced my
wonderful secret identity as a black-card-carrying zombie of
the Army of the Living Dead, expecting to get my jollies
watching her freak.

Only she didn't. She smiled at me. She fuckin' kissed me,

47

and she told me I was doin' the Work of Our Lady whether I knew it or not.

Say what? Say who?

And she told me.

She told me that whether I knew it or not, I was a soldier in a different army now, an army called the Lovers of Our Lady. Whose mission it was to have meat with as many people as possible in order to save the species, if you can believe *that* one, brothers and sisters! That somehow by all of us Giving as many strains of It to each other as we could, we might end up with multiimmune humans.

Believe it when they tell you L.A. is full of all kinds of weirdos, brothers and sisters!

But soon the weirdness began getting ominous. All of a sudden the SPs were swarming all over the meatbars like flies on horseshit, running every last customer they caught through the national data bank no matter how long it took. The underground safe houses were no longer so safe. They were grabbing people at random on the streets and blowing away anyone who showed any resistance. I mean, suddenly the Sex Police were real agitated.

I never did find out whether they were hot after me and my fellow zombies or what, I mean after a few close calls, there was clearly no percentage in sticking around to find out. Especially since the pallies were starting to wear off once more and I was getting to lookin' obvious and ragged. San Francisco was beginning to look like my best bet again after all.

I snatched me another car and headed north again, staying away from the population centers, meatfucking my way slowly up the center of California, following a kind of secret underground circuit.

It was real easy, once I got the hang of it and picked up on the stories. That weirdo back in L.A. had given me a good steer. All I had to tell these assholes was that I was doin' the Work of Our Lady and they'd do me anything.

DR. RICHARD BRUNO

IT WAS ARDUOUS, BUT MY LITTLE DREADNAUGHT WAS READY WITH
five days to spare, and it was even more elegant than my
original concept. Like the Plague itself, it infected via the
usual sexual or intravenous vectors, colonizing semen, blood,
and mucous membrane. Unlike the Plague, however, it did
not interfere with T-cell activity or production. Lacking an
antigen coat, it was "invisible" to the host immune system.

As a retrovirus, it would write itself into host genomes,
so that when it expressed itself during cellular reproduction,
it would invade two more cells, a process that would continue until all suitable host cells were infected.

If an invading retrovirus should be encountered during
the expression phase, it would destroy the active core and
wrap itself in the "dead" antigen coat. If the host already
had antibodies to these antigens, that variant would die. If
not, it would eventually write itself back into a host genome,
shedding the antigen "shell" in the process.

Thus, when a retrovirus invaded the host, the host bloodstream would become saturated with empty invader antigen coats, to which the host immune system would eventually form antibodies, conferring immunity to the invader precisely in the manner of a "killed virus" vaccine.

It not only conferred immunity to all strains of the Plague virus, it would automatically immunize the host against *all* retroviruses. And, like the Plague, it would spread via sexual contact.

That was what my molecular analysis predicted. It remained only to test the dreadnaught. But there was a stringent law against introducing into human hosts a live, genetically tailored organism capable of reproduction outside the lab, even for test purposes. It would take congressional legislation to allow me to begin human tests, and even then it could be years before the dreadnaught received FDA certification.

And I had only five days. In five days, I was up for ID card updating. If I tested out black, which I would, I would lose my job and be dumped unceremoniously into the San Francisco Quarantine Zone, and all would be lost.

I had only one chance to keep my blue card long enough to see the whole process through. I myself would have to be my first test subject. If it didn't work, all was lost anyway. If it did—and I was convinced it would—no one ever need know that I had violated the FDA regulations.

So I injected myself with the dreadnaught culture. Three days later, my body was free of the Plague. I took some of my blood and exposed it to other Plague strains as well as a variety of other retroviruses. My dreadnaught killed them all.

I called Harlow Prinz, the president of Sutcliffe, and asked for a special meeting of the board of directors, at which I promised to present the greatest advance in medicine in the last fifty years and then some. I could all but hear him drooling.

The Nobel for medicine seemed a certainty.

And, seeing as how the dreadnaught would spread itself by sexual contact without the need for economically prohibitive mass inoculation, it could eliminate the Plague from the festering Third World as well, so a second Nobel, this one for peace, might not be beyond the bounds of possibility.

WALTER T. BIGELOW

ELAINE REFUSED TO HAVE INTERFACE SEX WITH ME AT ALL. SHE refused to sleep in the same bedroom with me. She took to disparaging my manhood. Meals were undercooked, overcooked, slovenly prepared. Her housekeeping deteriorated. She kept insisting that I introduce Billy to the sex machine parlors and called my righteous refusal "un-Christian."

I no longer knew the woman I lived with. Elaine was now acting like a woman with a secret life, indeed like a woman hiding an adulterous relationship. Was it possible? How long had it been going on? Had she been making a fool of me all these years?

Of course I had the necessary resources to find out. I had her followed. But what the reports revealed was no human lover.

There were written accounts. There were still photos. There was even an ingeniously obtained clandestine video.

Elaine was a sex machine addict.

Almost every day when I was away at work, she visited one of several sex machine parlors, and stayed for at least an hour, engaging in machine sex perversions of which I had previously been unaware, which I had not even previously believed possible.

When I confronted her with the evidence, she defiantly admitted that she had been doing it secretly for years. "You just haven't been satisfying me, Walter."

"Adulteress!"

"*Adulteress?* Just the opposite! I've been doing it to *keep from becoming* an adulteress!"

"It's against God's law!"

"Show me anything in the scriptures against it!"

"It's the sin of Onan!"

"Good Lord, Walter, it's the Plague, can't you see that?"

"Of course I can see that! God is testing us, and you've failed Him."

"*I've* failed *Him?* Or has *He* failed *us?*"

"Blasphemy!"

"Is it?" she insinuated. "Can it be Jesus's God of Love who has taken natural love itself away from us and forced us into all these perversions? Look what's happened to us! Look what's happened to Billy! Where is God's Love in all that?"

"It's the Devil tormenting us, not God, Elaine!"

"That's what I'm telling you, Walter Bigelow! The Plague is the work of the Devil, not God. So anything that helps us survive Satan's torment—the interfaces, the sex machines—must be God's mercy. Jesus loves us, doesn't He? He can't want us to suffer any more than we have to!"

And then I knew for certain.

Not the Prince of Liars for nothing.

My Elaine had neither the evilness of spirit nor the cunning of mind to say these things to me. She was clearly possessed by the Devil.

Christian and husbandly duty coincided.

I placed Elaine under clandestine house arrest.

And began consulting exorcists.

DR. RICHARD BRUNO

THEY WERE ALL THERE—HARLOW PRINZ, THE PRESIDENT OF SUT-cliffe, Warren Feinstein, the chairman of the board, and the entire board of directors. They all had dollar signs in their eyes as I began my presentation. They listened with rapt silence as I proceeded, a silence that grew rather ominous and eerie as I went on.

And the conclusion of my presentation fell into a deathly graveyard hush that seemed to go on forever. I finally had to break it myself.

"Uh . . . any questions?"

"This, ah, dreadnaught virus is a self-replicating organism? It will reproduce by itself outside the lab?"

"That's right."

"And it spreads like the Plague?"

"It can easily enough be made pandemic."

"Who has had access to this information?"

"Why, no one outside this room," I told them. "I did this one on my own."

Like a crystal suddenly dissolving back into solution, the hushed atmosphere shattered into a series of whispered cross-conversations. After a few minutes of this, Prinz snapped orders into his intercom.

"Security to lab twelve! Seal it off. No one in or out except on my personal orders. Get a decontamination team down there and execute Code Black procedures."

"*Code Black?*" I cried. "There's no Code Black in my lab! No pathogen release! No—"

"Shut up, Bruno! Haven't you done enough already?" Prinz shouted at me. "You've created an artificial human parasite, you imbecile! The FDA will crucify us!"

"*If* we report it . . ." Feinstein said slowly.

"Yes . . ." Prinz said.

"What are you going to do, Harlow?"

"I've already done it. We'll follow maximum Code Black procedure. Incinerate the contents of lab twelve, then pump it full of molten glass. We'll keep this an internal matter. It never happened."

"But what about *him*?"

"Indeed . . ." Prinz said slowly. "Security to the board-room!" he snapped into his intercom.

"What the hell is going on?" I finally managed to demand.

"You've committed a very serious breach of FDA regulations, Dr. Bruno," Feinstein told me. "One that could have grave consequences for the company."

"But it's a monumental breakthrough!" I cried. "Haven't

you heard a word I've said? It's a cure for all possible Plague variants! It'll save the country from—"

"It would destroy Sutcliffe, you cretin!" Prinz shouted. "Fifty-two percent of our gross derives from Plague vaccines, and another twenty-one percent from the sale of palliatives! And your damned dreadnaught is a *venereal disease,* man—it wouldn't even be a marketable product!"

"But surely the national interest—"

"I'm afraid you haven't considered the national interest at all, Dr. Bruno," Feinstein said much more smoothly. "The medical industry's share of GNP has been twenty-five percent for years, and the Plague is hard-wired into our economy; your dreadnaught would have precipitated a massive depression."

"And destroyed the whole raison d'être of our policy vis-à-vis the Third World."

"Thereby shattering the Russian-Chinese-American-Japanese entente and rekindling the Cold War."

"Leading to a nuclear Armageddon and the destruction of our entire species!"

What monstrous sophistry! What sheer insanity! What loathsome utterly self-interested bullshit! They *couldn't* be serious!

But just then two armed guards entered the boardroom, and their presence suddenly forced me to realize just how serious the board really was. They were already destroying the organism. From their own outrageously cold point of view, their hideous logic was quite correct. The dreadnaught virus *would* reduce the medical industry to an economic shadow of its former self. Sutcliffe *would* fold. And their jobs and their fortunes would be gone. . . .

"Dr. Bruno is not to be allowed to leave the premises or to communicate with the outside," Prinz told the guards. They crossed the room to flank my chair with pistols at the ready.

"What are we going to do with him?"

How far would they really go to protect their own interests?

"Perhaps Dr. Bruno has met with an unfortunate accident in the lab . . ." Prinz said slowly.

My God, were they *deadly* serious?

"Surely you're not suggesting . . . ?" Feinstein exclaimed, quite aghast.

"The organism is being destroyed, we can wipe his research notes from the data banks, no one else knows, we can hardly afford to leave loose ends dangling," Prinz said. "You have any better ideas, Warren?"

"But—"

Did I panic? Did I become one of them? Was I acting out of ruthless self-interest myself, or following a higher imperative? Or all four? Who can say? All I knew then was that my life was on the line, that I had to talk my way out of that room, and the words came pouring out of me before I even thought them, or so it seemed.

"One million dollars a year," I blurted.

"What?"

"That's my price for silence. I want my salary raised to one million a year."

"That's preposterous!"

"Is it? You've said yourself that the survival of Sutcliffe is at stake. Cheap at twice the price!"

"Cheaper and safer to eliminate the problem permanently," Prinz said.

"Ye Gods, Harlow, you're talking about murder!" Feinstein cried. "Dr. Bruno's suggestion is much more . . . rational. He'd hardly be about to talk while we're paying him a million a year for his silence!"

"He's right, Harlow!"

"The other's too risky."

"I don't like it, we can't trust—"

"He'll have to agree to accept an appointment to the board," Feinstein said. "Meaning that he knowingly accepts legal responsibility for our actions. Besides, we're destroying the organism, aren't we? Who would believe him anyway?"

"Will you agree to Warren's terms?" Prinz asked me.

I nodded silently. In that moment, I would have agreed to *anything* that would let me get out of the building alive.

Only later, driving home, did I ponder the consequences of what I had agreed to, did I consider what on Earth I was going to do next. What could I possibly tell Marge and Tod? How could I explain our sudden enormous riches?

And what about my mission, my Hippocratic oath, my duty to suffering humanity? Those imperatives still existed, and the decision was still in my hands. For what the board fortunately did not know was that the dreadnaught virus had *not* been completely destroyed. The sovereign cure for the Plague was still alive and replicating in my body. I was immune to all possible Plague variants.

And that immunity was infectious.

JOHN DAVID

I MADE MY WAY UP THE COAST TO THE BAY AREA, AND THERE I WAS stymied, brothers and sisters. I kept on the move—San Jose, Oakland, Marin County, and back again in tight little circles. The SPs were everywhere, they were really paranoid, they were rounding up people at random on the street, and it wasn't only the likes of me they were after.

The Word had come down from the usual somewhere to put the heat on. The SPs around the meatbars were tighter than a ten-year-old's asshole. Everyone they rousted got their cards run through the national data bank, I mean there were roadblocks and traffic jams ten miles long. People were disappearing wholesale. And the poop in the underground was that they were doing all this to come down as hard as they knew how on anyone "doing the work of Our Lady."

And that was me, brothers and sisters. I mean, I was determined to meatfuck anything I could anyway, and calling myself a "Lover of Our Lady" was not only the best come-on line anyone had ever invented, it was ready access to the safe houses that were opening up everywhere in response to the heat, to cheap and even free pallies, to the whole black-carder underground. For sure, I'm not saying that I bought any of that bullshit about sacred duty to evolve immunity into the species, but I sure dished plenty of it out when it made life easy.

But why did I stick around the Bay Area in the middle of the worst Sex Police action in the country when sooner or later I figured to get caught in a sweep? When I did, and my phony blue card came up null, they'd run a make on my prints and come up with my Legion record, and then they'd for sure flush me down their toilet bowl, you better believe it!

Well, for one thing, the marks were coming out again, I was beginning to get moldy and obvious, and here at least I had some chance of disappearing into the underground. And for another, I was getting weak and feverish and maybe not thinking too clearly.

And there was San Francisco, clearly visible across the Bay. Where the SPs never went. The only safe place for a wanted zombie like me. The only place I could bop till I dropped. Sitting there staring me in the face. Somehow, getting there had become a goal in itself, something I just had to do before I went under. What else was left?

But there was an impenetrable line of razor wire and laser traps and crack SP troops across the Peninsula behind it and a bay full of pig boats patrolling its coastline and enough gunships buzzing around it day and night to take Brazil. All designed to keep the meatfuckers inside. But just as effective in keeping the likes of me out.

No one ever got out of San Francisco. And there was only one way in. Your card came up black, and the SPs loaded you into a chopper and dumped you inside from five feet up. But if the SP ever got its meathooks on me, they'd punch my ticket for sure, and not for San Francisco, you better believe it!

The only other way in was a loner kamikaze run on the blockade, and that was even more certain death. Oh yeah, I knew I was deep into Condition Terminal now, but *that* spaced-out yet, I wasn't!

DR. RICHARD BRUNO

WHAT I DID, FOR THE TIME BEING, WAS NOTHING. I BANKED MY NEW riches in a separate account and told Marge nothing. I showed up at the lab every day and puttered around doing nothing.

I staggered around in a trance like a moral zombie, hating myself every waking moment of every awful day. I had successfully performed my life's mission. I had conquered the Enemy. I could have been the Savior of mankind. I *should* have been the Savior of mankind.

Instead, all I could do was hide the secret from my wife and collect my blood money.

Would I have done it on my own? Would morality finally have been enough? Would I have ultimately been faithful to the oath of Hippocrates? I would never know.

My son Tod took the decision out of my hands.

One night the Sex Police showed up at our house with Tod in custody. He had been caught in a raid on a meatbar.

His card had come up blue against the national data bank and he had passed a spot genome test that I had never heard of before, so they really had nothing to hold him for.

But they read Marge and myself the riot act. This kid was caught peddling his ass in a meatbar, we don't know how long he's been doing it, he claims it was his first time. He's blue now, but you know what the odds are. Get the horny little bastard an interface and scare the shit out of him, or he's gonna end up as Condition Terminal in San Francisco.

While Marge broke down and wept, I had my awkward man-to-man with Tod, poor little guy. "Do you realize what you've been risking?" I demanded.

He nodded miserably. "Yeah," he said, "but . . . but isn't it worth it?"

"Worth it!"

"Oh, Dad, you knew what it was like, flesh on flesh without all this damned metal and rubber! How could you expect me to live my whole life without ever having that?"

"It's your *life* we're talking about, Tod!"

"So what!" he cried defiantly. "We're all gonna die sooner or later anyway! I'd rather live a real life while I can than die an old coward without ever knowing anything but interfaces and sex machines! I'd rather take my chances and be a man! I'd rather die brave than live like . . . like . . . like a pussy! Wouldn't you?"

What could I possibly say to that? What would *he* say if he knew my wonderful and awful secret? How could I even look my own son in the eye, let alone continue this lying lecture? What could I possibly do now?

Only one thing.

If I was still too much of a cowering creature to save the

world at the expense of my own life, at least I could contrive to save my son, and without alerting the powers at Sutcliffe in the process. And at least covertly pass this awful burden off to someone else.

Tod's plight had shown me the way and given me the courage to act.

A stiff dick might ordinarily know no conscience. But mine was the exception that proved the rule. It *was* my conscience now. *Use me,* it demanded. *Use me and let a Plague of life loose in the world.*

LINDA LEWIN

"I MAY BE A MEATWHORE, BUT I'M NOT A MONSTER!" I TOLD HIM indignantly. "What you're asking me to do is the most loathsome thing I've ever heard!"

He had approached me in a meatbar in Palo Alto.

I had been spending a lot of time in such places lately, for here the Work of Our Lady was doubly important. For here bitter and twisted black-carders came with their phony blue cards to take sexual vengeance on foolish blue-carders. Every time I could persuade one of these wretches to take their comfort in me, I saved someone from the Plague. And every time I could persuade him afterward to do the Work of Our Lady instead of infecting more blue-carders, the ranks of the Lovers of Our Lady grew.

But Richard, as he called himself, was something different, the lowest creature I had ever encountered even in a place like this.

He wanted me to have meat with him, and then, a week

later, to have meat with his own teenage son! And I could name my own price.

"What's so terrible about that?" he said ingenuously. "Your card will come up blue, won't it?" But his sickly twisted grin told me all too well that he knew the truth. Or part of it.

I knew what a chance I was taking. He could be under-cover SP. He could be anything. But if I just refused and walked away, he'd only find another meatwhore with a phony blue card more than willing to take his money to do this terrible thing.

"I'm *her*," I told him. "I'm Our Lady of the Living Dead."

He didn't even know who Our Lady was or the nature of the Work we were doing. So I told him.

"And that's why I won't do what you ask. I only have sex with black-carders. I've Got It. And I'll give the Plague to you and your son. And so would any meatwhore you're likely to find. Don't you really know that?"

"You don't understand," he insisted. "How could you? You can't give me the Plague, no one can. I'm immune."

"You're *what*?"

And he told me the most outrageous story. He told me that he was Dr. Richard Bruno of the Sutcliffe Corporation, that he had developed an organism that conferred immunity to all Plague variants. That he could infect me with it and make me a carrier. That's why he wanted me to have meat with his son, to pass this so-called dreadnaught virus to him.

"You really expect a girl to believe a line like that?"

"You don't have to believe anything now," he told me. "Just have meat with me now; you've already Got It, so you have nothing to lose. A week later, meet me here, and I'll take you to a doctor. We'll do a full workup. If you test out blue, you'll know I'm telling the truth. I'll give you fifty thousand right now, and another fifty thousand after you've had meat with Tod. Even if I'm lying, you're still a hundred thousand richer, and you've lost nothing."

"But if you're lying to me, I'll have given you the Plague!" I told him. "I won't risk that."

"Why not? I'm the one taking the risk, not you."

"But—"

"You *do* know what I'll do if you refuse, don't you?" he said, leering at me. "I'll just offer someone with less scruples the same deal. Even if I'm just a lying lunatic, you won't have saved anyone from anything."

He had me there. I shrugged.

"I've got a room just around the corner," I told him.

DR. RICHARD BRUNO

IT WAS THE BEST SEXUAL EXPERIENCE I'VE EVER HAD IN MY LIFE, or at any rate since my teenage years, back before the Plague. Flesh on flesh with no intervening interface or rubber, and with no fear of infection either, the pure simple naked act as it was meant to be. And while some part of me knew that it was adultery, an act of disloyalty to Marge, a better and higher part of me knew that it was an act of loyalty to a higher moral imperative—to Tod, to suffering humanity— and that only sharpened my pleasure.

But I did feel shame afterward, and not for the adultery. For *this,* this pure simple act of what was once quite ordinary and natural pleasure, was what I had the power to bring back into the world, not just for me and for her and for Tod, but for everyone everywhere. This was my victory over the Enemy. And what was I doing with it?

Nothing. I was taking a million dollars a year's blood

money to hold my silence and, admittedly, to preserve my own life.

But now that I had already taken the first step upon it, a way opened up before me. I could hold my silence and keep taking the money, but I could spread the dreadnaught virus far and wide, via this cult of Our Lady and my own clandestine action.

The moral imperatives of the oath of Hippocrates and the fondest desire of any man coincided. It was my duty to have meat with as many women as I could as quickly as possible.

LINDA LEWIN

I HADN'T EVEN DARED TO LET MYSELF *WANT* TO BELIEVE IT, BUT OH God, it was true!

The underground doctor to whom Richard Bruno had taken me ran antibody tests and viral protein tests and examined blood, mucus, and tissue samples through an electron microscope.

There was no doubt about it. I was free of all strains of the Plague. Indeed, there was not a retrovirus of any kind in my body.

"Do you know what this means?" I cried ecstatically on the street outside.

"Indeed I do. The long nightmare of the Plague Years is coming to an end. We're carriers of life—"

"And it's our duty to spread it!"

"First to my son. Then to as many others as quickly as possible. We need to infect as many vectors as we can before

. . . in case . . . so that no matter what happens to us . . ."

I hugged him. I kissed him. In a way, in that moment, I think I began to love him.

"When?" I asked him breathlessly.

"Tonight. I'll bring him to your room."

DR. RICHARD BRUNO

TOD WAS ALL HOT SWEATY EXCITEMENT WHEN I TOLD HIM I WAS
taking him to a real human whore. "Oh Dad, Dad, thank
you . . ." he cried. But then he hesitated. "This girl . . . I
mean, you're sure she's . . . you know . . ."

Now *I* hesitated. Between telling him the easy lie that I
had found him a real blue-carder or telling him the whole
improbable truth. I sighed. I screwed up my courage. I had
lived too long with deception.

"It's really true?" Tod said when I had finished. "The
dreadnaught virus? What they did at Sutcliffe? All that
money?"

I nodded. "Do you believe me, Tod?"

"Well yeah . . . I mean I want to, but . . . but why haven't
you told Mom? Why haven't you . . . you know, given it to
her?"

"Would she have trusted me?"

"I dunno . . . I guess not. . . ."

74

"Do *you* trust me?"

"I want to . . . I mean . . ." He looked into my eyes for long moments. "I guess I trust you enough to take the chance," he finally said. "I'm the one that did all the talking about being brave, huh, Dad. . . ."

I hugged my son to me. And I took him to Linda Lewin's room. He entered tremulously but he stayed almost two hours.

LINDA LEWIN

I LONGED TO SHOUT THE GLORIOUS TRUTH FROM THE ROOFTOPS, BUT when Richard told me the whole horrible story of what had happened at Sutcliffe, I had to agree that I should continue the Work of Our Lady as before, spread the dreadnaught virus as far and wide as possible among the unknowing before those who would stop us could find out what was happening. It was hard to believe that such greedy evil was possible, but the fact that I was cured and the world knew nothing about the dreadnaught proved the sad truth that it was.

Richard swore Tod to secrecy too, and together and separately the three of us began to spread the joyful infection around Palo Alto, telling no one.

Why did I stay in Palo Alto for two weeks instead of resuming my usual rounds up and down California, when in fact spreading the cure around the state as quickly as possible would have probably been wiser and more effective?

Perhaps I felt the need to be near the only two people who shared the glorious secret and the deadly danger of discovery. Perhaps I had fallen in love in a strange way with Richard, with this tormented, fearful, but oh so brave man.

More likely that I knew even then in my heart of hearts that this couldn't last, that sooner or later Sutcliffe would get wind of it and we would have to run. And when that happened, Richard and Tod would be helpless naïfs without me. Only Our Lady would have the connections and road wisdom to even have a chance to keep them one step ahead of our pursuers.

DR. RICHARD BRUNO

ONCE AGAIN, WHAT COULD I POSSIBLY TELL MARGE? THE WHOLE story, including the fact that my Hippocratic oath required me to have meat with as many anonymous women as I could? That I had our son similarly doing his duty to the species?

Obviously I had been inexorably forced step-by-step into such extreme levels of marital deception that there was no way I could now get her to believe the truth, let alone accept its tomcatting moral imperative.

Yet, tormented as I was by the monstrous series of deceptions I was forced to inflict upon my wife, I had to admit that I was enjoying it.

After all, no other men in all the world had the possibility of enjoying sex as Tod and I did. Meat on meat as it was meant to be, and not only free of fear of the Plague, but knowing that we were granting a great secret boon with our favors, that we were serving the highest good of our species in the bargain.

And I was cementing a unique relationship with my son. Tod and I became confidants on a level that few fathers and sons achieve. Swapping tales of our sexual exploits, but sharing the problem of how to recruit Marge to the cause too.

Or, at the very least, infect her with the dreadnaught. But Marge would never have meat with me. Nor would she willingly abandon monogamy. Sexually, psychologically, Marge was a child of the Plague Years, and even if she were to be convinced of the whole truth, she would never condone the need for my profuse infidelities, let alone agree to spread the dreadnaught in the meatbars herself.

In retrospect, of course, it was quite obvious that things could not really go on like this for long.

They didn't.

Tod got caught in an SP raid on a meatbar again.

But they didn't drag him home this time. Instead, the news came on the telephone, and it was Marge who chanced to take the call. Tod was being held at the Palo Alto SP headquarters. Other detainees had told the SP that he had been a regular. Black-carders had admitted having meat with him. He was undergoing testing now and his card was sure to come up black.

"Don't worry," I told her when she relayed this information in a state of numb, teary panic, "they'll have to let him go. He'll test out blue, I promise."

"You're crazy, Richard, that's plain impossible! You're out of your mind!"

"If you think I'm crazy now," I said, pouring her a big drink, "wait till I get drunk enough to tell you why!"

I gulped down two quick ones myself before I found the

courage to begin, and kept drinking as I babbled out the whole story.

"Now let me give the dreadnaught to you," I woozed when I was finished, reaching out for her in a state of sloppy inebriation.

She shrieked, pulled away from me, ran around the living room screaming, "You animal! You're crazy! You've killed our son! Stay away from me! Stay away from me!"

How can I explain or excuse what happened next? I was drunk out of my mind, but another part of me was running on coldly logical automatic. If there could be such a thing as loving rape, now was the time for it. Marge was certain that I was a sinkhole of the Plague, and there was only one way I could ever convince her of the truth. I had to infect her with the dreadnaught, and I couldn't take no for an answer.

The short and nasty of it was that I meatraped my own wife, knowing I was doing the right thing even as she fought with all her strength against me, convinced that she was fighting to keep herself from certain infection with the Plague. It was brutal and horrible and I loathed myself for what I was doing even as I knew full well that it was ultimately right.

And left her there sobbing while I reeled off into the night to retrieve Tod from the SP.

I was in a drunken fury, I was a medical heavyweight, I demanded that they run a full battery of tests on Tod and myself, and I browbeat the tired SP timeserver who ran them unmercifully. When they all turned out blue, I threatened lawsuits and dire political recriminations if Tod were not released to my custody at once, and succeeded thereby in deflecting his attention from the "anomalous organism" he had noticed in our bloodstreams long enough to get us out the door.

But the "anomalous organism" would be noted in his report. And Sutcliffe would be keeping close tabs on my data file, and there were certainly people on their end who would put one and one and one together. It was only a question of how much time it would take.

And we couldn't stay around to find out. We had to run. Tod, myself, Linda, and Marge. But where? And how?

We drove to Linda's and had to wait outside for half an hour till the man she was with left.

LINDA LEWIN

"THERE'S ONLY ONE PLACE WE CAN GO," I TOLD TOD AND RICHARD. "Only one place we can hide where the SP can't come after us . . ."

"The San Francisco Quarantine Zone?" Richard stammered.

I nodded. "The SP won't go into San Francisco. There isn't a Fuck-Q alive who'd be willing to do it."

"But . . . *San Francisco* . . . ?"

"Remember, *we* have nothing to fear from the Plague," I told them. "Besides . . . can you think of anywhere where what we three have is more needed?"

"But how can we even *get* inside the Zone?"

I had to think about that one for a good long while. I had never even heard of anyone trying to get past the SP *into* San Francisco. On the other hand, neither had the SP. . . .

"Our best bet would be by boat from Sausalito. We wait for a good foggy night, then cross the Golden Gate through the fog bank in a wooden rowboat, no motor noise, no radar profile. The patrol boats stick in close to San Francisco and they're watching the coastline, not the Bay. The helicopters won't be able to see us through the fog even if they are flying. . . ."

"Sounds like risky business," Richard said dubiously.

"Any better ideas?"

Richard shrugged. "Let's go collect Marge," he said.

DR. RICHARD BRUNO

THE THREE OF US PILED INTO LINDA'S CAR—THEY'D BE LOOKING for mine once they were looking for anything—and drove back to our house.

Marge was still in a state of shock when we got there. Even when she saw Tod, even when he and Linda backed up my story, she still couldn't quite believe me. She started to come around a bit when I showed her the enormous balance in my secret account.

But when I told her we had to flee to San Francisco, she fell apart all over again. There was no time for further persuasion. Tod, Linda, and I were forced to wrestle her into the car by brute force, with my hand clamped over her mouth to prevent her from screaming.

We drove around the rim of the bay to Sausalito, bought a rowboat, rented motel rooms, and waited.

The fog didn't roll in good and thick until two nights

later. During these two days, with Tod and Linda and myself talking to her almost nonstop, Marge slowly came to believe the truth.

But accepting the fact that all of us had a moral duty to spread the dreadnaught in the only way possible was a bit more than she could swallow. She could accept it intellectually, but she remained emotionally shattered.

"I believe you, Richard, truly I do," she admitted as the sun went down on our last day in Sausalito. "I can even admit that what you're doing is probably the right thing. But me, I just can't. . . ."

"I know," I told her, hugging her to me. "It's hard for me too . . ." and I made tender love to her, meat on meat as it was meant to be, for what was to prove to be the last time.

That night a big bank of fog rolled in through the gap in the Golden Gate Bridge, a tall one too, that kept the gunships high above the San Francisco shoreline. It was now or never.

Tod hesitated on the pier.

"Scared?"

He nodded.

"Me too, Tod."

He clasped my hand. "I'm scared, Dad," he said softly. "I mean, I know we don't have much of a chance of making it. . . . But if anything happens . . . I want you to know that I wouldn't have it any other way. . . . We had to do what we did. I love you, Dad. You're the bravest man I've ever known."

"And I'm proud to have you for a son," I said with tears in my eyes. "I only wish . . ."

"Don't say it, Dad."

I hugged him to me, and then we all piled into the boat, and Tod and I began to row.

The currents were tricky and kept pushing us east and the going was tougher than I had anticipated, but we steered for the lights of the city and made dogged progress.

We couldn't have been more than five hundred yards from the shore when a spotlight beam suddenly pinned us in a dazzling circle of pearly light. "Rowboat heave to! Rowboat heave to!"

So near and yet so far! If the SP caught us, we were finished. We had no choice but to row for it.

We pulled out of the spotlight and zigged and zagged toward the shore while a motor roared back and forth behind us and the spotlight flitted randomly over the flat waters. The fog was quite thick, and they had trouble picking us up again.

When they finally did we were within two hundred yards of the shore. And then they opened up with some kind of heavy machine gun.

"We're sitting ducks in this boat!" Tod shouted. "Got to swim for it!" And he dived overboard and down into the darkness of the waters under a hail of bullets.

Everything seemed to happen at once. The boat tipped as Tod dived, Linda rolled over the side, Marge panicked and fell overboard, the boat turned turtle—

And we were all in the cold water, swimming as far as we could under water before surfacing for air, catching quick breaths, swimming for our lives beneath a random fusillade of bullets and a skittery searchlight beam.

There was no room for thought or even fear as I swam for

my life with aching lungs, no time or space to feel the horror of what was happening. Until, gasping for air, exhausted and freezing, I clawed my way up a rocky beach.

Out across the dark waters, the searchlight still roamed and the machine-gun fire still flashed and chattered. Linda Lewin crawled up beside me, panting and coughing. We lay there, not moving, not talking, not thinking, for a long time, until the gunboat finally gave up and disappeared into the fog.

Then we got up and searched the beach for at least an hour.

Tod and Marge were nowhere to be found.

"Maybe they made it farther up the beach," Linda suggested wanly.

But I knew better. I could feel the void in my heart. They were gone. They were gone, and I had killed them as surely as if the hand on the machine-gun trigger had been mine.

"Richard—"

I pulled away from her comforting embrace.

"Richard—"

I turned away from her and let a cold black despair roll like a fog bank into my mind, erasing all thought, and filling me with itself, wondering whether it would ever roll out again.

And hoping in that endless bleak moment that it never would.

JOHN DAVID

I SUPPOSE I KNEW IT HAD TO HAPPEN SOONER OR LATER, BROTHERS and sisters, but at least I thought I'd be able to go down fighting and take some of the meatfuckers with me.

It didn't happen that way. They got me while I was asleep, would you believe it!

I was going downhill fast, I was feverish, weak, and I wasn't really thinking, I mean I was wandering the streets like an obvious zombie for real. I got picked up by some people whose faces I don't even remember who took me to an Our Lady safe house in Berkeley, where I passed out as soon as I hit the mattress.

Some meatfuckin' safe house!

I got woke up in the middle of the night by a gun butt in the back of the neck and another in my belly. They rounded everyone in the joint up and hauled us to the SP station. They ran everyone's cards against the national data bank.

Everyone but me. Me, they didn't have to bother, seeing as I was an obvious Condition Terminal and they had caught me with about a dozen assorted phony blue cards in my kit. Me, they just took my finger and retina prints and faxed 'em to Washington.

"Well, well, well," the SP lieutenant purred after no more than half an hour. "John David, recently of the Legion, wanted for about ten thousand counts of murder, meatrape, and ID forgery, not to mention robbery, insurrection, border crashing, and treason. You're a bad boy, aren't you, John? But I'm real pleased to meet you. I get the feeling you're gonna get me a nice promotion. Tell you what, if you do, the night before they do you, your last meal's on me."

WALTER T. BIGELOW

NOT CONTENT WITH POSSESSING MY WIFE, SATAN PURSUED ME TO my office. First the blasphemous cult of Our Lady and then a series of anomalies in the San Francisco Bay Area that seemed to indicate that the national data bank had somehow been compromised.

It was common enough for phony blue cards to come up black against the national data bank. But it was unheard-of for anyone caught with a forged blue card not to prove out black upon actual testing for the Plague, for of course it made absolutely no sense for someone with a valid blue card to use a forged one.

But it was happening around the Bay Area. There were almost a dozen cases.

And now this truly bizarre incident last night in the same locale. Four people in a rowboat had actually tried to run the Quarantine blockade *into* San Francisco! Two of them seemed to have actually made it.

When the bodies of the other two were fished out of the Bay, they proved to be Tod and Marge Bruno, the son and wife of one Dr. Richard Bruno, a prominent genetic synthesizer with the Sutcliffe Corporation.

The local SP commandant was due for a promotion or at least a commendation.

He had run all three names through the national data bank. Tod Bruno had been caught in a meatbar sweep three days previously. Although many witnesses claimed he was an habitué, he had come out blue under a full spectrum of tests. The commandant had had the wit to dig deeper and found that some "anomalous organism" had been noted in the actual report.

Instinct had caused him to order the bodies of Tod and Marge Bruno to be given a thorough and complete autopsy down to the molecular level. And it was that report that put me on a plane for San Jose.

There was a strange "pseudovirus" written into both of their genomes. It shared many sequences with the Plague virus but resembled no known or extrapolated variant, and it had other sequences that could not have evolved naturally. The bodies had been dead too long to try to culture it.

An unknown "pseudovirus" in the bodies of the family of a prominent genetic synthesizer . . . It could only be one thing—an unreported Condition Black incident at Sutcliffe. And the ultimate handiwork of the Devil had been released—some kind of horrible artificial human parasite, a manmade Plague variant. We had two corpses that had been infected with it, and I was virtually certain that Bruno at least was also infected, and was alive somewhere in San Francisco.

What might happen in that cesspit of Satan was none of my affair, but Tod Bruno had been infected when he was picked up in a meatbar outside the Quarantine Zone, and he had passed through a full battery of tests and come out blue.

Meaning that this monstrous thing was invisible to all our standard Plague tests. What had the Devil wrought at the Sutcliffe Corporation?

As I flew westward, I had the unshakable conviction that I was flying toward some climactic confrontation with the Adversary, that the battle of Armageddon had already begun.

LINDA LEWIN

SAN FRANCISCO WAS NOT WHAT I HAD EXPECTED. I'M NOT SURE WHAT I had really expected, a foul Sodom of ruins and rotting zombies, maybe, but this was not it.

The streets were clean and the quaint buildings lovingly cared for. The famous old cable cars were still running and so were the buses. The restaurants were open, the bars were crowded, and there were cabarets and theaters. There were even friendly cops walking beats.

Food and various necessities were allowed in through the Daly City Quarantine Line and sterilized products allowed out, so the city did have an economy connected to the outside world. The place was poor, of course, but the people inside it held together to see themselves through. Food was expensive in the restaurants but artificially cheap in the markets. Housing was crowded, but the rents were kept low, and the indigent or homeless were put up in public buildings and abandoned BART stations.

Oh yes, there were many horrible Condition Terminals walking around, but many more people who could have easily melted into the underground life outside. And there was something quite touching about how all the temporarily healthy deferred to and showed such tender regard for the obvious Living Dead, something that reminded me of dear old Max.

Indeed his spirit seemed to hover over this doomed but fatalistically gay-spirited city. Of necessity, everyone was forced to be a Saint Max here, and although the Lovers of Our Lady did not exist as such, everyone here seemed to be doing the Work.

No one here had to worry about Getting It, or being carded, or picked up by the SP. All of that had already happened to all of them. So, while there were more open gays here than I had ever thought to see in my life, stranger still to say, there was less . . . perversion in San Francisco than anywhere else I had ever been.

No meatbars as such, for every bar was a meatbar. Hardly any sex machine parlors, for the people of San Francisco, already all under sentence of death, could give one another love freely, like what natural men and women must once have been. Even the obviously terminal had their needs tenderly cared for.

No place I had ever been seemed more like home.

Only the pall of Plague that hung over the city marred the sweetness of the atmosphere, and that seemed softened by the fogs, pinkened by the sunsets, lightened by the death-house gaiety and wistful philosophic melancholy with which the citizens confronted it. "Everyone's born under a death sentence anyway," went the popular saying. "Here at least we all know it. There is no tomorrow sooner or later, so why not live and love today?"

Uncertain of what to do next, I began doing the Work of Our Lady in the usual manner, offering myself to anyone and everyone, spreading the dreadnaught slowly, but unsure as to whether or when to spread the glorious news.

I would have been happy there—indeed the truth of it was that I *was* happy—even while I sorrowed for poor Richard.

Richard, though, was like a little child whom I had to lead around like a creature in a daze. All his energy and motivation seemed to have vanished with his wife and son. I could understand his grief and guilt, but this couldn't last forever.

"We've got work to do, Richard, glorious and important work," I kept telling him. "We've got to spread the dreadnaught among these people."

Mostly, he stared at me blankly. Sometimes he managed a feeble, "You do it."

After a few days of this, I decided that I could no longer wait for Richard to come around. I had to make the fateful decision on my own.

This spreading the dreadnaught by myself clandestinely was just too slow. If there were evil men out there intent on stopping the dreadnaught, they'd be tracking us down. I needed to infect thousands, tens of thousands, before they could act, and the only way that could happen would be if the people of San Francisco *knew* what they were spreading and set out to do it systematically.

First I began revealing myself as Our Lady to my lovers and in the bars, and there were enough people in San Francisco who had once done the Work on the outside—even some I had once known in my circuit-riding days—so that my claim gained credibility.

In one sense, the people of San Francisco had always been doing the Work of Our Lady, of Saint Max, but in another sense, the legend had never been central here. In San Francisco, the people did the Work of Our Lady to please one another and themselves, not because they believed they were serving the species' only hope.

But then I began recruiting an army of Lovers of Our Lady and I did it by proclaiming the glorious truth.

That the shattered man I sheltered in my rooms was a great scientist and an even greater hero. That he had developed the dreadnaught organism. That through him I had been infected with the gift of life. That I could infect anyone I had meat with with the cure, that anyone I had meat with would also become infectious. That the Plague Years, through Richard Bruno's instrumentality and at horrible personal cost to himself, were now coming to an end.

That all we had to do was what we were doing already—love one another.

There were more skeptics than believers at first, of course. "Bring me your Terminals," I told them. "Let them have meat with Our Lady. When they're cured, the whole city will see I'm telling the truth."

WALTER T. BIGELOW

SATAN HIMSELF SEEMED TO BE SPEAKING THROUGH HARLOW PRINZ when I confronted him, laughing his final laugh, for what the president of Sutcliffe finally admitted under extreme duress was worse, far worse, than what I had originally feared.

Bruno had been working on some sort of Plague-killer virus. But he had been building it around a Plague variant and something went wrong. He had created instead a Plague variant that mutated randomly every time it reproduced. That was invisible not only to all current tests short of full-scale molecular analysis, but would *remain so* to anything that could be devised.

There *had* been a Condition Black, but only inside the lab, and there were plenty of reports to prove that Sutcliffe had followed proper procedure, as well as a mountain of legal briefs supporting the position that such internally contained Condition Blacks need not be reported to the SP.

"We had no idea Bruno was infected," Prinz claimed. "Isn't that right, Warren?"

Warren Feinstein, Sutcliffe's chairman, who had sat there silently all the while with the most peculiar expression on his face, fidgeted nervously. "No . . . I mean yes . . . I mean how can we be so sure he *was* infected . . . ?"

"The man's wife and son were infected, now weren't they, Warren?" Prinz snapped. "You heard the director. Extreme measures must be taken at once to contain this thing!"

"But—"

"Wait a minute!" I cried. "Surely you're not suggesting the man . . . had *meatsex* with his wife and . . . and his *son* knowing he was infected?"

"Let's hope so," Prinz said. "At any rate, we have no choice but to act on that assumption."

"What?"

"Because if he didn't . . ." Prinz shuddered. "If he didn't, then we may all be doomed. Because if Tod and Marge Bruno *weren't* infected sexually, then this new virus has to be what we've always feared most—a Plague variant that doesn't need sexual or intravenous vectors, an ambient version that spreads through the air like the common cold."

"Oh my God."

"You have no alternative, Mr. Director," Prinz went on relentlessly. "You must obtain the necessary authority from the president and have San Francisco sterilized at once."

"Sterilized?"

"Nuked. Condition Black procedure, admittedly on a rather extreme scale."

"That's monstrous, Harlow!" Feinstein shouted. "This is going too far! We've got to—"

"Shut up, Warren!" Prinz snapped. "Consider the alternative!"

Feinstein slumped over in his chair.

"If this thing *is* ambient, we're all doomed anyway, so what's the difference?" Prinz said in Satan's cold, insinuating voice. "But if it isn't, and if Bruno's spreading it in San Francisco . . ."

"You can't just kill a million people on the supposition that—"

"Shut up, Warren!" Prinz snapped. "You can't afford to listen to this sentimental fool, Mr. Director. You've got to be strong. You've got to do your duty."

My duty? But where did that lie? If I had the San Francisco Quarantine Zone sterilized by a thermonuclear explosion, Bruno would be vaporized. And I had to have Bruno live for interrogation before I did any such thing, I realized. I had to know whether he had had meatsex with his wife and son. For if he had, then I would know the virus *wasn't* ambient, that there was hope. *Then* and only then could I have San Francisco sterilized with a clear conscience.

Then and only then would such an awful decision serve God and not the Devil.

I had to find someone willing to go into San Francisco and bring Bruno out. But where was I going to find someone crazy or self-sacrificing enough to do that?

JOHN DAVID

I WAS FEELING PRETTY PUNK WHEN TWO SPS DRAGGED ME INTO AN interrogation room, handcuffed me to a chair bolted to the floor, and then split.

But I came around fast, you better believe it, when old Walter T. himself walked into the room and shut the door behind him!

The old meatfucker came right to the point.

"I've been looking for someone very special, and the computer spit your name out," he told me. "I've got a job for you. Interested?"

"You gotta be kidding. . . ."

"We're going to drop you in San Francisco. I want you to bring a man out."

"Say what?" Well, shit, brothers and sisters, I could hardly believe my ears. I mean, even in my present Condition Terminal, my ears pricked up at *that* one. And old Walter T., he sure didn't miss it.

100

"Interested, aren't you? Here's the deal. . . ."

And he told me. An SP helicopter would drop me into San Francisco, where I was to snatch and hold this guy Richard Bruno. Every afternoon at three o'clock they'd have a chopper circle Golden Gate Park for an hour. When I had Bruno, I'd shoot off a Very pistol, and they'd pick me up.

"What do you want this guy for?" I demanded.

"You have no need to know," he told me.

I eyed him dubiously. "What makes you think I'll want to come out?" I mean, this dumb meatfucker was gonna throw me into my briar patch, but what could possibly make him believe I'd do his dirty work for him and deliver some poor bastard to the SP? Could he *really* be as stupid as he seemed? It didn't seem real likely.

"Because upon delivery of Bruno you'll be given a full pardon for all your capital crimes."

"Hey, look at me, man, I've got maybe a month left anyway."

"You can go back into the Legion. As a captain."

"As a captain?" I snorted. "Shit, why not a bird colonel?"

"Why not indeed?"

"You're really serious, aren't you?" Jeez, what a tasty run I could have as a fuckin' brigade commander. But . . . "But I'm a goner anyway. What difference is it gonna make?"

"The Legion is going into Brazil again even as we speak," he told me. "We can pump you up with the best military pallies and all the coke and speed you can handle. And drop you into Brazil with colonel's wings at the head of a brigade twelve hours after you deliver Bruno. A short life, but a happy one."

"Terrific," I said, studying old Walter T. carefully. This

still didn't quite add up. He was holding something back, and I had a feeling I wasn't gonna like it. "But what makes you so sure I wouldn't prefer to spend that short happy life in San Francisco?"

Now it was Walter T.'s turn to study *me* carefully, then shrug. "Because unless you bring Bruno out, that could be a lot shorter than you think."

"Huh?"

"We're going to drop you into San Francisco anyway, so I might as well tell you the truth," Bigelow said. "I get the feeling nothing else is really going to motivate you, but *this* surely will."

He told me, and it did.

Bruno was some kind of genetic synthesizer. He had screwed up real bad and created a new Plague variant that was invisible to all the standard tests and just might be able to spread through the air.

"So we need to know whether Bruno is infected with something that could be spreading around San Francisco right now, something that we can only hope to stop by . . . shall we say measures of the maximum extremity."

Well, brothers and sisters, I didn't need any promotion to bird colonel to figure out what he meant by *that*. "You mean nuke San Francisco, don't you?"

"Unless we have Bruno to examine and unless that examination reassures us that he hasn't been spreading this thing, we really have no alternative. . . . I'll give you two weeks. After that, well . . ."

"You nuke San Francisco with me inside it!"

Bigelow nodded. "I think I can trust you to do your honest best, now, can't I?" he said.

Well, what could I say to that? Only one thing, brothers and sisters. What I told old Walter T. next.

"I want the coke and the speed and the pallies *right now.* All I can carry."

"Very well," he said. "Why not? Anything you need."

"I don't have any choice, now, do I?"

"None whatever."

If I hadn't been cuffed to the chair, I would have ripped off the old meatfucker's arm and beaten him to death with it. But even then, I had to admire his style, if you know what I mean. Turn the bastard's card black, and old Walter T. would have been right at home with us fellow zombies.

LINDA LEWIN

AFTER THE MARKS STARTED TO FADE FROM TERMINAL CASES AND
black-carders started proving out blue on the simple tests
the underground docs put together, the word began to
spread faster, and so did the dreadnaught, and the Lovers of
Our Lady began to spread the good news on their own in
the streets and bars of San Francisco.

One day a delegation came to me and took me to a ram-
bling old house high on a hill above Buena Vista Park that
they called the House of Our Lady of Love Reborn. They
installed me in quarters on the third floor and they brought
Richard with me.

There I was surrounded by the Lovers of Our Lady. And
so was Richard. He was surrounded by people who cared for
him, who loved him, who knew what heroic deeds he had
done, and at what terrible cost. Slowly, far too slowly, he
began to react to his surroundings, to mutter haltingly of
his guilt and despair. But he still refused to join in the

Work, for he found the mere thought of sex loathsome, no matter who offered themselves to him, including myself.

And the Work itself, though proceeding apace, was going far too slowly. How long did we have before the outside world learned the truth? Months? Weeks? Days? And what would happen then? Indeed, might it be in the process of happening already?

What I needed to do was infect all of San Francisco with the dreadnaught, so that when the outside world finally intruded, it would be presented with the truth and its massive proof as a glorious fait accompli—an entire city, a Quarantine Zone once completely black, now entirely free of the Plague.

Once, long before most of the people here were born, San Francisco had experienced a magical few months that was called the Summer of Love, a legend that still lived in the myth of the city.

So I conceived the notion of a Week of Love, a celebration of the dreadnaught and a means of quickly spreading it to all, a carnival of sex, a citywide orgy, a festival of Our Lady of Love Reborn.

And perhaps via such a manifestation and celebration of what he had brought back into the world, Richard too might be reborn back into it. . . .

JOHN DAVID

THE PALLIES THEY SHOT ME UP WITH BEFORE THEY DROPPED ME IN San Francisco didn't seem to do much good, but the speed and coke sure did, brothers and sisters. I might look like Condition Terminal on its last legs, but I was riding high and burning bright on the way out, you better believe it!

I expected San Francisco to be weird and wild, something like TJ before the SP moved in on us, but this was something else again, weird for sure, but not exactly this zombie's idea of *wild.*

The city was like something out of an old movie—clean, and neat, and like you know *quaint,* like some picture post-card of itself, and I found I could have just about any kind of meat with anyone I wanted to just by asking for it, even looking like I did.

There were plenty of terminal zombies like me walking around and plenty more outrageous faggots, but these people were like so damned sweet and kind and nicey-nice to us on the way out it made me want to puke. I mean all this peace and sympathy sex and love pissed me off so bad I just about *wanted* to see Wimp City nuked, if you know what I mean.

But not, of course, with me in it!

Bigelow had it covered. I had no choice at all. I had to get my crumbling ass in gear and get my mitts on Bruno, on my only ticket out.

DR. RICHARD BRUNO

I CAN HARDLY REMEMBER WHAT IT WAS LIKE INSIDE THAT PLACE OF darkness or even precisely how and when I began to emerge from it. First there was a soft warm light in my cold blackness, and then I slowly began to take notice of my surroundings.

I was living in an ancient Victorian house high on a hill in San Francisco, a place that was known as the House of Our Lady of Love Reborn. Linda Lewin was living there with me, and I knew that she had been caring for me through my long dark night. As had many others. For this was a house of love and hope. It was a kind of brothel, and a kind of church, and what was being spread here was my dreadnaught virus. And all those who came and went here loved me.

"Dr. Feelgood," they all called me. Not the creature who had brought his wife and son to death, but the man who had brought love back into the world.

"You've grieved long enough, Richard; Marge and Tod

are gone, and they deserve your grief," Linda told me. "But you've also done a wonderful thing, and that deserves your joy. Come join the party now. See what they died for. See what you've brought back into the world! This is the Festival of Our Lady of Love Reborn, but it's the Festival of Dr. Feelgood, too."

And she and the Lovers of Our Lady took me on a tour of San Francisco, on a tour of the carnival, on a tour through an erotic wonderland out of long-lost dreams.

The whole city was partying—in the bars and the parks and the streets. It was Mardi Gras, it was the feast of Dionysus, it was the Summer of Love, it was beautiful madness. Everyone was drunk and stoned and deliriously happy, and people were making love, sharing meat, openly everywhere—in apartments, in bars, right out on the streets.

They were celebrating Love Reborn in the very act of creating it. They were celebrating the end of the Plague Years as they brought it to an end with their joyful flesh.

"Do you understand, Richard?" Linda asked later, back at the house of Our Lady of Love Reborn. "Marge and Tod are dead and they never lived to see what they died for, and that's a sad thing, and you're right to mourn. But they didn't die in vain, they died to help you bring love back into the world, and if they're watching from somewhere, you can know they're smiling down on you. And if they're not, if there's no God or Heaven, well then, we're all we've got, and we can only take shelter in the living. Do you understand?"

"I'm not sure, Linda . . ." I murmured.

"Then let me help you to begin now," she said, holding me in her arms. "Come take shelter in me."

And, hesitantly at first, but with a growing strange peace in my heart, a warrior's peace, a peace that had become determination by the time we had finished our lovemaking, I did.

And afterward, I understood. Marge and Tod were gone and nothing I could do would bring them back, and that was a terrible thing. The Plague Years had in one way or another made monsters and madmen of us all, we had all been trapped into grievous mistakes, fearful, and frustrated, and loathsome acts, and nothing we did now could change that either. We had *all* been victims, and perhaps the lives of all of us who lived through the Plague Years could never be made whole.

But that dark night was ending and a new day was dawning, and we, and I, had to act to give it birth and protect it into its full maturity. My personal life had died back there in San Francisco Bay with Marge and Tod and I had nothing left but my duty to the Hippocratic oath.

And vengeance.

Nothing I could do would ever bring my family back or entirely erase my guilt in their deaths. But I could take my vengeance on Prinz, on Feinstein, on the Sutcliffe board, I could do my part in seeing to it that their worst fears were realized, that the dreadnaught virus they had sought to destroy spread far and wide, saving suffering humanity while it destroyed the Sutcliffe Corporation in the process.

Thus would my part in the twisted nightmare of the Plague Years end with the ultimate perverse yet joyful irony:

Just and loving vengeance.

So tomorrow I will go forth into San Francisco and join the Week of Love. And tonight I am sitting here in the

House of Our Lady and writing my story in this journal, which is now concluding. When it is finished, it will be sent to the president, to the head of the Federal Quarantine Agency, to the news services, to the television networks. Before you let them act against us or tell you that this is all an evil lie, demand that they go in and test the populace or at least a good sample for Plague. That's all I ask. Know the truth for yourself. Tell others.

And I promise it will set all of you free.

JOHN DAVID

I HAD GOOD PHOTOS OF BRUNO, BUT YOU EVER TRY TRACKING DOWN one guy in a city of a million? Especially in a city that seemed to have gone completely apeshit. Everyone seemed to be drunk or stoned. People were having meat *everywhere* right out in the open, in the streets, in the parks, in alleys. Half-dead as I was, they were still shoving their meat even at the likes of me, babbling a lot of crazy stuff about how they were saving me from the Plague, as if anything could help me now!

I was goin' out fast, I was a mess of sarcomas and secondary infections, weak, and feverish, and half out on my feet, taking enormous doses of speed and coke just to keep going. But, fast as I was going, I still knew that this city was gonna go faster, and with me in it, unless I could deliver Bruno to the SP. I mean, one way I had maybe three weeks left, the other only ten days.

An extra eleven days of life may not seem like such a

big deal to *you,* brothers and sisters, but it sure as shit would if *you* were the one who knew that was the best you had left!

Anyway, it was enough to keep me focused on finding Bruno, even spaced and stoned and dying and staggering around in the biggest orgy the world had ever seen. And I started grilling random people on the street and being none too gentle about it.

I was so far gone I must have beaten the crap out of half a dozen of them before it got through to me that the "Dr. Feelgood" the whole damn city was babbling about was the very guy I was looking for. Dr. Richard Bruno, the son of a bitch who had maybe let loose the worst Plague variant ever and who for sure was gonna get all these assholes vaporized, and me with them; and they were somehow convinced the bastard was some kind of hero!

Well, after I copped to that, it wasn't much sweat tracking the famous Dr. Feelgood down. All I had to do was follow my nose and all the talk about him through the bars and streets until I ran into someone who told me he was partying in a certain bar in North Beach right now.

I got there just as he was walking out with a good-looking momma on his arm and a dreamy smile on his lips. As soon as I saw him, I went into motion, no time or energy left for tactics or thought.

"Okay, Bruno, you son of a bitch, you're comin' with me!" I shouted, grabbing him by his right arm and whipping it behind his back into a half-nelson bring-along.

Half a dozen guys started to move in, but, far gone as I was, I still had that covered. I already had my miniauto out and waving in their faces.

"This guy's comin' with me, assholes!" I screamed. "Anyone tries to stop me gets blown away!"

Then everything seemed to happen at once.

Some jerk got brave and slammed into my knees from behind.

I kicked blindly backward, fighting for balance.

Bruno yanked himself out of the half-nelson.

A circle of angry meat closed in.

I started firing without caring at what, whipping the miniauto in fanning fire at full rock and roll.

"Dr. Feelgood" got himself neatly stitched up the back from ass to shoulder by high-velocity slugs.

Bruno folded as everyone else came down on me like a ton of bricks.

Next thing I knew, I had had the shit thoroughly beaten out of me, and two guys were holding me up by the shoulders, and Bruno was down there on the sidewalk croaking and looking up at me.

"Why?" he whispered with blood drooling out of his mouth.

"Don't die, you stupid meatfucker!" I screamed at him. "You're my only ticket out of here!"

"Kill the bastard!"

"Tear him apart!"

I laughed and laughed and laughed. I mean, what else was there to do? "Go ahead and kill me, suckers!" I told them all. "I'm dead already and so are you, gonna nuke you till you glow blue!"

"Cut his heart out!"

Bruno looked up at me from the sidewalk with this weird

sad little grin, almost peaceful, kind of, as his light went out.

"No . . ." he said. "No more . . . just and loving vengeance, don't you see . . . Marge . . . Tod . . . it's nobody's fault . . . take him . . . take him. . . ."

His voice started to fade. He coughed up more blood.

"Take him where, Richard?" a woman said, leaning over him.

"Take him to Our Lady . . ." Bruno whispered. "Let him take shelter in . . . in . . ."

His lips moved but no more sound came out. And that was the end of that.

Bruno was dead.

So was I.

And in ten days, so was San Francisco.

LINDA LEWIN

THEY BROUGHT RICHARD'S BODY BACK TO THE HOUSE OF OUR LADY
of Love Reborn and laid him out on a couch. Half a dozen
Lovers of Our Lady were restraining a wild-eyed young terminal case and being none too gentle about it.

And they told me what had happened. And Richard's
dying words.

Only then did I really look at his murderer. His body was
a mass of sarcomas. His frame was skeletal. His eyes were
red and wild.

"Why?" I asked him in a strange imploring voice that
surprised even me.

"My ticket out of here before they drop the Big One, Lady
but it's all over now ain't it do your damnedest we're all
dead zombies anyway brothers and sisters. . . ."

He wasn't making sense, nor would he, I knew then. This
poor creature was no more responsible for his actions than
Richard had been when Marge and Tod died. I had heard of

this sort of thing before. Condition Terminals turning berserker on the way out, taking as many as they could with them. He too was a victim of the Plague, as were we all.

And I understood Richard's last words now too, perhaps better even than he had in the saying of them. His life had been in a sense over already, and all this poor creature had done was set his tormented soul free. I understood why he had forgiven his assassin, for in that act of forgiving, he had at last found forgiveness for himself for the deaths on his own hands, or so at least I prayed to whatever gods there be.

"What should we do with the bastard?"

"Kill him!"

"Tear his damn heart out!"

"No!" I found myself saying. "I'll do it for you, Richard," I whispered, and I took his murderer's hand. "He forgave you, and so must I."

"Go ahead and kill me, don't want your forgiveness, it don't mean shit, I'm a dead man already and so are you!"

"No, you're not," I told him gently. "Let me take you upstairs and give you the good news."

JOHN DAVID

AND SHE DID, THOUGH OF COURSE I DIDN'T BELIEVE A WORD OF IT at the time, not even after Our Lady gave my disgusting dying flesh the gift of her meat. Not that I was exactly in any mental condition for deep conversation anyway.

But days later, when the sarcomas began to disappear and my head cleared, I knew that the whole damn story that Linda had told me over and over again was all true.

I mean, I had sure done my share of evil, but what those meatfuckers at Sutcliffe had done was enough to make a combat medic puke! I never had no use for Walter T. Bigelow—and less so after the number he had run on me—but I was willing to bet that the old meatfucker had believed what he told me about poor Bruno. Those Sutcliffe creeps must have fed him their line about Bruno to get him to nuke the evidence of what they had done out of existence. And the dreadnaught virus along with it! Just to line their own pockets and save their own worthless asses!

And oh shit, Bigelow still believed it!

"What day is this?" I asked Linda when my head was finally clear enough to realize what all this meant and what was about to happen.

It was two days till the Big Flash.

"You've given me the good news, now I've gotta give you the bad news," I told her. And I did.

I had never seen Our Lady break down and cry before, but now she did. "Then poor Richard died for nothing. . . . And everyone here is doomed. . . . And no one will even know. . . . And the Plague will go on and on and on. . . ."

While she was moaning and sobbing, I did some fast thinking. I still had the Very pistol, and that SP chopper was going to circle Golden Gate Park at three for two more days. I had the means to bring it down, and if I could take it . . .

"You gotta find me a guy who can fly a helicopter," I said.

Our Lady stared at me blankly. I shook her by the shoulders. "Hey, you gotta snap out of it, Linda, and listen to me! I got a way to get us out of here before they drop the Big One!"

That brought her around, and I laid it out for her.

It was simple, really. We'd dress the helicopter pilot up in a trench coat and a slouch hat or something so no one could see he wasn't Bruno until I got us aboard the SP chopper.

"I'll take care of the rest," I promised. "Probably be just a pilot and a copilot, piece of cake. Then you come aboard, and we take off like a big-assed bird for the Marin side, ditch the chopper, and disappear. You saved my life, now I'll save yours."

LINDA LEWIN

"BUT WHAT ABOUT *SAN FRANCISCO*?" I SAID. "WE CAN'T JUST . . ."

John shrugged. "San Francisco is gonna be nuked out of existence anyway," he said. "Nothing we can do about that, our asses is all we can save."

"But all these people . . . and the dreadnaught virus . . ."

"Look at it this way—at least there'll be you and me left to spread it. . . ." He leered at me wolfishly. "I'll do my part to spread it far and wide, you better believe it, sister!"

"We just can't leave a whole city to die!"

"You got any better ideas?"

I stared at this poor savage creature, at this killing machine, at this ultimate victim of the Plague, and I thought and thought and thought, and finally I did.

"We'll capture the SP helicopter," I told him. "But we won't just escape. We'll fly down to Sutcliffe—"

"And do what?"

"Capture Harlow Prinz and Warren Feinstein. Take them to Bigelow."

"Huh?"

"Don't you see? When they tell Bigelow the truth—"

"Why the hell would they do that?"

I did my best to imitate John David's own fiercest leer. "I think I can leave that one up to you, now can't I?" I said.

He stared at me as his face slowly twisted into the mirror image of my own. "Yeah . . ." he said slowly. "I think I could enjoy that. . . ."

He frowned. "Only this is getting mighty dicey, sister. I mean, grabbing the chopper should be no sweat, and if all we was doing was putting it down in Marin and disappearing on foot, our chances would be pretty good. But faking the radio traffic long enough to fly the thing to Palo Alto and snatching the Sutcliffe creeps and getting them to Bigelow . . . Hey, the SP ain't the Legion, but they ain't that far out to lunch either. . . ."

"We've got to try it!"

"We wouldn't have a chance!"

"What if we had a diversion?" I blurted. "A big one . . ."

"A diversion?"

My blood ran cold as I said it. It was monstrous. Thousands might die. But the alternative was a million dead for no good cause. And monstrous as it was as a tactic, it was still the only just thing to do. Morally or practically, there really was no choice. It was the only chance we had to save the city, and the people had the right to know.

"What do you think would happen if everyone in San Francisco knew what you've just told me?" I said.

"That they were all going to be nuked in two days? Are you kidding? They'd go apeshit! They'd—"

"Storm the Quarantine Line en masse? Swarm out into the Bay in hundreds of small boats? Try to get across the gaps in the bridges?"

"Jeez, it'd be just like TJ, only a thousand times bigger, the SP would have its hands full, we just might be able to. . . ."

He studied me with new eyes. "Hey, beneath all that sweetness and light, you're pretty hard-core, you know that, sister? I mean, using *a whole city* as a diversion . . ."

"These people have a right to know what's going to happen anyway, don't they, John?" I told him. "Wouldn't *you* want to know? This way, even if we fail, they get to go out fighting for something and knowing why. Better in fire than in ice."

WALTER T. BIGELOW

SATAN HELD ME ON THE RACK AS I WAITED FRUITLESSLY FOR DAVID to extract Richard Bruno from San Francisco. Three and four times a day Harlow Prinz called me to demand in shriller and shriller tones that I have the city nuked. Was this the voice of God or the voice of the Devil? What did Jesus want me to do?

And then Satan put my back to the final wall.

Reports started coming in to the Daly City SP station, where I had ensconced myself, that a huge ragtag flotilla of small boats was leaving the San Francisco shoreline. Fighting had broken out all along the landward Quarantine Line.

It was becoming all too apparent that I could procrastinate no longer.

Mobs with bridging equipment were swarming onto the San Francisco ends of the Golden Gate and Oakland Bay bridges. The whole city was trying to break out of the Quarantine Zone, and they couldn't all be stopped by conventional means. Only a thermonuclear strike could prevent the new and far deadlier Plague strain from entering the general populace now.

I was forced to put in my long-delayed fateful call to the president of the United States. . . .

JOHN DAVID

I HAD WANTED THE BIG BREAKOUT TO START SHARPLY AT THREE TO
make damn sure the SP chopper wasn't scared off, but Linda
had told too many people, and the Lovers of Our Lady were
out in the streets whipping things up for hours beforehand,
and the action began to come down raggedly an hour early.

But the fighting was going on at the borders, not the
center, and Golden Gate Park was just about empty. The SP
chopper pilot must've been over the city already, or maybe
he was the sort of righteous asshole who followed the last
order no matter what.

For even with half the city already throwing itself against
the Quarantine Line, the chopper appeared over the park
right on the money at three sharp.

I fired off the Very pistol, and down it came. I stuck my
miniauto conspicuously in our pilot's back and frog-marched
him to the open chopper door.

As I had figured, there were only a pilot and a copilot in

the cockpit. The moment we were inside, I jammed the muzzle of my piece into the back of the pilot's neck.

"Outside, assholes!" I ordered. "But strip first! One word out of either of you and I blow you away!"

"Hey—"

"What the—"

"I told you, no lip! Out of those uniforms! Move your asses!"

They took one look at the miniauto and another at me, and stripped down to boxer shorts and T-shirts muy pronto, you better believe it!

"Out, assholes. Better run till you drop, and don't look back!"

I booted them out of the chopper and fired a long burst over their heads as Linda climbed aboard, and they ran for the nearest bushes.

Then me and our pilot put on their uniforms, which I figured would come in mighty handy if we ever made it to Sutcliffe, and off we went.

The skies were empty as we headed south over the city at about three thousand feet, but things started getting hairy as we approached the Quarantine Line.

I could see ragged mobs of people moving toward the SP positions below, the SP troops were using heavy machine guns and some light artillery, and the air beneath us was thick with gunpowder smoke, through which I could see sparkles, laser-straight tracers, occasional explosions.

All hell was breaking loose on the ground, and the airspace below us was full of helicopter gunships making low, slow strafing runs with cannon and rockets.

But all the thunder and lightning and confusion made it

easier for us in the end, seeing as we were one chopper out of many.

"Bravo five three seven Charlie, what the hell are you doing up there?" a voice screeched at us over the radio.

"Don't answer!" I told our pilot. "Take her down into the traffic!"

When we had dropped down into the cloud of gunships, I screamed into my microphone, "Motherfucking black-carder faggot bastards!" And fired off a few rockets.

"Hey, those are *our* people down there!"

"And *our* asses up *here*! You just fly this thing, and let me worry about tactics, okay!" And I fired off a couple more blind shots into the confusion.

It worked like a charm. Every time we got static on the radio, I cursed and screamed like a good combat animal and fired a few random rockets at the ground and nobody challenged us as we threaded our way south over the combat zone.

Once we were well clear, we went back up to three thousand feet, and the only traffic we saw between Daly City and Palo Alto was a few more gunships heading north into the mess far below who probably didn't even see us.

We landed inside the Sutcliffe compound right in front of the administration building and sat there with our rotor whumping as company rent-a-cops poured raggedly out of the building and finally managed to get us surrounded.

"Stay here, and fer chrissakes keep the engine running," I told Linda and the pilot. And climbed out of the chopper to make like a modern major general.

"National Emergency!" I barked at the bozo in charge of the rent-a-cops. "Direct orders from Walter T. Bigelow, director of the Federal Quarantine Agency. He wants Harlow Prinz and Warren Feinstein in his headquarters half an hour ago, and we're here to get 'em!"

"Hey, I got no orders to—"

"Argue with Bigelow if you want to!" I snapped. I gave the sucker a comradely shrug. "But I don't advise it. I mean, there's already been some kind of screw-up over this with all the heat going on, and he ain't exactly being reasonable just now, if you get me."

"I don't take my orders from the SP!"

"Your funeral, pal," I told him, nodding toward the chopper. "I got orders to blow the shit out of this place if I meet any resistance, and there's five more gunships orbiting just over the ridgeline in case you got any dumb notions . . ."

"Hey, hey, don't get your balls in an uproar," the head rent-a-cop soothed much more politely, and trotted off into the building.

I waited there outside the chopper surrounded by rent-a-cops for what seemed like ten thousand sweaty years but couldn't have been more than ten minutes by the clock.

Finally the head rent-a-cop appeared with two middle-aged bozos. One of them seemed to be staggering toward me in a daze, but the other was the sort of arrogant in-charge son of a bitch you want to kill on sight.

"What's the meaning of this?" he screamed in my face. "I'm Harlow Prinz, I'm the president of this company, and I don't—"

"And I'm just Walter Bigelow's errand boy, but I don't take shit either," I told him. "Except of course from the boss man, and I got enough of that for being late already! So do us both a big favor and get into this chopper." I waved my miniauto. "'Cause if you don't, shit is about to flow down-hill, if you get my meaning."

The wimpy type, who had to be Warren Feinstein, started to climb aboard, but that murdering meatfucker Prinz stood there with his hands on his hips looking suspicious. He took a good long look at my badly fitting uniform. "Let's see your papers," he said.

I brought up the muzzle of my piece and pointed it at his belly button. "You're lookin' right at 'em," I said.

"Harlow, for chrissakes, he *means* it!" Feinstein said, and hustled his ass into the copter.

Prinz moved slowly past me to the door and reluctantly started to board the chopper, but he must've spotted Linda when he peered inside and put it all together.

'Cause he suddenly aimed a sloppy kick at my nuts that missed the target but knocked me off balance, yelled, "Shoot! Shoot!" at his rent-a-cops, and broke and ran.

Furious as I was, I didn't blow my combat cool.

I leaped through the door, scattering the rent-a-cops with a long fanning burst as our pilot lifted the chopper, and flipped myself into the copilot's seat.

By this time we were about a hundred feet in the air, and heading straight up into the wild blue yonder.

"Hold it right here a minute!" I told the pilot.

The rent-a-cops were scattering for cover. Only a few of 'em had the balls to fire a few useless shots up over their shoulders and they plinked harmlessly off the chopper's armored belly.

Prinz was running for the administration building. I smiled. I lined the bastard up in my sights and savored it just for a moment. This, after all, was the son of a bitch who was willing to let the Plague take us all to line his own pockets. I had wasted more citizens than I could count, but this was going to be special. This was going to be primo.

"Thanks ever so much for making my day," I told Harlow Prinz as he reached the stairs leading up to the entrance. And I fired a single rocket.

A perfect shot. It hit him right in the base of the spine and blew him to dogmeat.

I went aft, where Feinstein was cowering against a bulkhead. I grabbed him by the neck with my left hand, squeezed his jaws open, and jammed the muzzle of my piece down his throat.

"You saw what I did to your buddy," I told him. "And knowing what I know about you sons of bitches and what you've done, you better believe I enjoyed it just as much as I'll enjoy wasting *you* if you don't do exactly what you're told. Get the message, meatfucker?"

Feinstein nodded and I pulled the gun barrel out of his mouth. And when I tossed his worthless ass onto the deck, he just lay there blubbering. "I *told* Harlow he was going too far, it's not my fault, it wasn't my idea, Bigelow will believe me, won't he, I swear I'll tell him the truth, I never thought, I never knew. . . ."

"He *better* believe you, meatfucker, or a lot of asses are gonna be grass," I told him. "And *you* better believe that you're gonna go first!"

WALTER T. BIGELOW

THE STATION WAS IN AN UPROAR. THE SITUATION WAS GROWING
graver by the minute. The mob had bridged the gap in the
Golden Gate and fighting was raging on the Marin side of
the span. Our gunboats were sinking scores of small craft
loaded to the gunwales with black-carders, but all was chaos
on the Bay; they couldn't establish or hold a line. The landward Quarantine Line was crumbling under human wave
onslaughts.

There was no alternative. When I got the president on
the line I was going to have to ask him to authorize an
immediate nuclear strike against San Francisco.

But while I was waiting for my call to the White House
to get through, there was a commotion in my outer office,
and a moment later an SP captain burst inside.

"Warren Feinstein's outside, Mr. Director," he stammered. "There's . . . there's a girl with him who says she's
Our Lady of Love Reborn . . . and there's a man holding him

at gunpoint. Says he's gonna blow his head off if we make a move and—"

There was a further commotion in the outer office and then Feinstein was rudely thrown through the doorway by a man who held the barrel of a miniauto at the back of his neck, followed by a young girl, and half a dozen SP men with drawn pistols.

The man with the miniauto was John David, whom I had sent into San Francisco after Richard Bruno. And he was wearing an SP uniform.

"What's the meaning of this?" I demanded. "This isn't Bruno! How did you—"

"No shit!" David snarled, prodding Feinstein with his gun barrel. "Go ahead, tell the man, or I'll blow your worthless head off!"

Tears poured from the eyes of Sutcliffe's chairman as he blubbered out the most incredible and chilling story.

"Harlow *lied* to you, Bruno's virus wasn't an ambient Plague variant, it was a *cure* for all Plague variants, an artificial venereal disease—"

"A *cure*? But then why—"

"—that conferred total immunity—"

"If it was a cure, then why on Earth did you suppress it?" I shouted at him. "Why did you tell me—"

"It's a venereal disease!" Feinstein babbled. "Spreads by itself, nothing for us to market, it would have bankrupted Sutcliffe, brought on an economic depression, Harlow insisted—"

I could not believe my ears. I could not be hearing this. "You suppressed a total cure for the Plague to preserve your own profits? My God, Prinz kept trying to get me to nuke San Francisco *just to keep Sutcliffe solvent?*"

Feinstein shook his head. "By then it was too late, don't you see?" he moaned. "The whole thing had gone too far. I warned him, I swear I did, but he insisted that San Francisco *had* to be nuked to cover up what we'd done. . . ."

Feinstein seemed to pull himself together with an enormous effort. "But you can't do that now," he said much more coherently. "You won't do that now. I'm willing to take my medicine, even if it means spending the rest of my life in jail. Harlow was wrong, monstrously wrong, and I was weak, horribly weak. You can't nuke San Francisco. You can't kill millions of people. You can't destroy the dreadnaught virus."

Was this the truth, or was it Satan's greatest lie? Feinstein was, after all, speaking with a gun at his throat. And he was a self-admitted liar.

If this was the Devil speaking through him, and I believed Satan's greatest lie, I would infect the nation with a deadly new Plague variant that might destroy all human life.

But if God had chosen this unlikely instrument to reveal His truth at the eleventh hour and I *didn't* believe it, I would not only be responsible for the deaths of a million people, I would be responsible for destroying God's own cure for the Plague.

What was I to do? What could I believe? *Whatever* the truth was, Satan could not have devised for me a more perfect moral dilemma.

"The president on the line . . ." said a voice on my intercom.

No man should be forced to make such a decision. But I

was. And I had to do it now. But I could not. There was only one thing that I could do.

There, in front of Feinstein, and David, and my own men, and with the president of the United States waiting on the telephone, I sank unashamedly to my knees and prayed aloud.

"Please, Jesus, I know that this cup cannot pass from me," I prayed. "But grant me at least one mercy. Send me a Sign. Show me Your Countenance."

And God, in His infinite wisdom, answered my prayer, through the most unlikely of instruments.

The young girl stepped forward. "Let me help you," she said softly. She took my hand in hers and raised me to my feet. "Let me be your Sign," she said.

"*You?* You're—"

"Our Lady of Love Reborn—"

"—the blasphemous mouthpiece of Satan!"

"No, I'm not. Nothing speaks through me but the truth in an ordinary girl's heart, and I'm very much afraid," she said with the strangest gentleness. "But I know that this man is speaking the truth, and there's no one else. So I *have* to be your Sign, now don't I? In the only way I can."

"How?" I asked softly, wanting very much, in that moment, to believe. In Jesus. In God's Grace. In anything that would show me the truth.

Even in she whom I had believed to be my nemesis, even in Our Lady of Love Reborn, if she could make me.

"By placing my life in your hands," she said.

I locked eyes with Our Lady of Love Reborn. They were young and they were fearful, but there was a strength in them too that seemed timeless. She smiled the Madonna's smile at me. Or was this only what I was longing to see?

"There's a helicopter waiting outside. I'm going to go to it and fly back to San Francisco. If the city dies at your hand, so will I. Would Satan's mouthpiece do that, Walter Bigelow?"

"The president on the line . . ."

"You would do that?" I said. "You'd really do that?"

She nibbled nervously at her bottom lip. She nodded demurely. "You'll have to kill me right now to stop me," she said, letting go of my hand and turning to confront the men blocking the doorway. "Will you tell these men to shoot me, Mr. Bigelow? Or will you let me pass?"

JOHN DAVID

"HEY, LINDA, YOU CAN'T DO THAT, WE'RE SAFE HERE, DON'T BE crazy!" I said, grabbing her by the arm.

The SP guards trained their pistols on us, looking to Bigelow for orders. I brought up my miniauto, flipped it to full rock and roll as conspicuously as I could, just daring the mothers to try it.

"I can, John, I must," Linda told me, and took two steps forward with me hanging on to her.

I turned to confront Bigelow. I could see that he *wanted* to believe. Wouldn't you?

What can I tell you, brothers and sisters? Maybe I figured Bigelow needed a final push. Anyway, how could I let her do this thing all alone? A short life, but a happy one, as we say in the Army of the Living Dead.

"Not without me, you don't," I said, taking her hand.

"The president on the line . . ."

I whipped the miniauto around and pointed it right at

Bigelow's head. "I could blow you away right now," I told him. "And don't think I wouldn't enjoy it, meatfucker!"

Walter T. Bigelow looked straight into my eyes and didn't flinch. The bastard had balls, you had to give him that.

"But I won't," I told him. " 'Cause this old zombie believes her. And you've gotta believe her too."

"Make me," Walter T. Bigelow said softly. "I truly pray that you can."

"Then try *this*," I said. I smiled, I shrugged, and I threw the miniauto on the floor in front of him. "We're gonna walk out of here to that helicopter, and we're gonna fly back to San Francisco. You can clock us on radar."

I turned to face the pistols of the SPs. "Or you can have these bozos fill us full of holes—your choice, Bigelow," I said over my shoulder. "Of course then you'll never know, now will you?"

And hand in hand we walked toward the armed men blocking the doorway.

The guards' fingers tightened against their triggers.

The moment hung in the air.

"Let them pass," Walter T. Bigelow said behind us. "Praise the mysterious workings of the Lord."

WALTER T. BIGELOW

AND THE TWO OF THEM WALKED OUT OF THE ROOM HAND IN HAND toward the helicopter, toward San Francisco, toward their faith in the wisdom and mercy of God, which no true Christian, in that moment, could justly deny.

In all my life, no one had placed greater trust in me than this young girl and this savage young man.

A nimbus of clear white light seemed to surround them as they walked out the door, and there were tears in my eyes as I watched them go.

God could not have granted me a clearer Sign.

I sank once more to my knees and gave thanks for His infinite wisdom, His infinite mercy, for His presence in that room, in that moment, in my heart, for the Sign He had granted me in my ultimate hour of need.

The rest is, as they say, history, and this is the end of the story of my part in it.

I did not ask the president for a nuclear strike. Instead I

told him what Feinstein had told me. And I issued an order for my troops to cease firing, to let those seeking to leave San Francisco pass as well.

There was much confusion afterward as hundreds of thousands of people poured out of the San Francisco Quarantine Zone. Congress called for my impeachment. I offered up my resignation. It was refused. Proceedings began in the House.

But as the hearings began, hundreds of escapees from San Francisco were rounded up, and all of them tested out blue. And the dreadnaught virus was found in all of their bodies.

So did the Plague Years end. And so too my public life. I became a national hero once more, and though there was no further need for a Federal Quarantine Agency or its director, I could no doubt have been elected to any office in the land.

But I chose instead to retire. And write this memoir. And go off on a long retreat into the desert with my family to try to understand the mysterious ways of God. And to reconcile with my wife.

And God granted us an easy reconciliation, for Satan had gone from her, if he had ever really possessed her, and she believed in me again.

"It was a true Christian act, Walter, and a brave one," she told me the night she took me once more into her arms. "God works in mysterious ways."

So He does. And perhaps the true wisdom is that that is all we can ever really know of the workings of His Will.

Did Satan send the Plague to torment us? Or did God send the Plague to chastise and test us?

If so, it was a terrible chastisement and a cruel testing.

But so was the Great Flood, and the Ten Plagues, and the Forty Years in the Wilderness, and of course Jesus's own martyrdom on the Cross.

"Love thy neighbor as thyself," Jesus told us, and was crucified for it.

How could that be the Will of a God of Love?

How could the Plague Years be the Will of God either?

I don't know. I don't think I ever will.

And yet my faith is still strong. For God spoke to me in my greatest hour of need through the unlikely instrumentalities of a young girl whom I had believed to be Satan's daughter and a vicious creature who had certainly spent most of his life doing the Devil's work on Earth.

Such a God I will never understand.

In such a God I can only believe.

Such a God I can only love.

AFTERWORD

THE JOURNEY OF *JOURNALS OF THE PLAGUE YEARS* FROM INITIAL conception to this first freestanding book publication has been a long and strange one, mirroring our passage into the Plague Years themselves in some ways, foreshadowing it in others.

Back around 1986, I began to realize that AIDS was going to be more than a deadly new disease. A virtually universally fatal disease that spread by sexual contact would create, in fact had already created, a baleful new existential equation between sex and death, and that could not fail to alter our psyches and our society on the most intimate and ultimate of levels.

I began to study the scientific literature, to follow the unfolding exploration of the strange nature of the virus itself, the attempts to develop cures, palliatives, vaccines. I began to ponder the unfolding politics of the situation. I began imagining what it was like to enter puberty during these

Plague Years, never to have known an adolescent moment when unprotected natural sex was not linked with potential death.

The children of such Plague Years would not be like thee and me. There would be social and political consequences. The economic impact of the Plague would grow and grow. Already, religious fundamentalists of a certain extremist bent were talking of AIDS as God's judgment on sinners, as a vindication of their beliefs, and this marginal viewpoint was likely to move closer to the national front and center.

By sometime in 1987, I had decided that I wanted to write a novel on the subject, an exploration of a world after a full generation under the shadow of AIDS, and I was ready to write an outline to present to Bantam Books, my regular publisher.

My agent was somewhat less than encouraging.

"Forget it," she told me. "You write great outlines, but no matter how good your outline is, no publisher will touch it with a fork. Because they know the distributors will shun it like the, uh, plague, too."

She believed that the subject was too frightening, that the public was in too deep a state of denial, out of which they had no desire to be roused, for a speculative novel about AIDS to be commercially viable; she believed, at the very least, that the publishing industry was convinced that this was true.

To me, perversely enough, this only confirmed the conviction that *Journals of the Plague Years* had to be written.

When she saw that I couldn't be talked out of trying, she implored me to at least keep the word *AIDS* out of the manuscript.

That concession to the publishing realities I did make on a conscious level. And in retrospect, I believe that I may have made a far greater concession on a subconscious level to the unfortunate commercial realities that, paradoxically, had a positive creative effect.

My customary method of writing novels is to write an outline first for both commercial and creative purposes. Commercially, an outline is something to show to a publisher in order to secure a contract. Creatively, the writing of the outline is where I first tell the story to myself, where I develop the structure, the settings, the characters and their voices.

From my occasional screenwriting work, I've learned to write these outlines for novels in the manner of treatments for film scripts, where the idea is not just to convey the plotline but to give a real feel for what the script and hence the potential film is going to be like.

Usually these novel treatments of mine run between twenty and forty pages. But as I started working on my treatment for *Journals of the Plague Years,* it started getting longer, and longer, and longer. I found myself writing whole short scenes, one after the other. I found myself putting in more and more detail, more and more of the thinking I had done about the disease and its possible cure.

By the time I had finished, to my own befuddlement and amazement, I had produced a treatment of well over a hundred pages, half the length of many whole books.

At the time, I believed that I had poured so much into this huge treatment because my agent had convinced me that *Journals of the Plague Years* was at best going to be a very difficult novel to sell to a publisher, that I had therefore better write the mother of all outlines to have any chance at all.

But looking back, I wonder.

I wonder if on some deeper subconscious level I hadn't believed what my conscious mind refused to believe—that my agent was right, that no matter what I wrote, no matter how good it was, in that time and place a novel like *Journals of the Plague Years* was simply going to be unpublishable. And that therefore, the outline was going to be all there was, that I had to get it all said there or not at all.

When my agent read *Journals of the Plague Years,* her opinion was that this was about the best novel outline she had ever read, but that the chances of selling the book it purported to describe were still zilch.

And she was right.

My editors at Bantam, Lou Aronica and Shawna McCarthy, rejected it as a proposal for a novel.

But in the same breath they told me that they wanted to publish *the outline itself* in *Full Spectrum,* an anthology they were putting together.

Say what?

The reading public is simply not ready for a novel like this, I was told, or at least we're not ready to risk trying to distribute it. But as part of a major anthology rather than a freestanding book, the commercial risk is minimal, and we're willing to take the chance.

Understand, I had never conceived of what I had shown them as something I had written for the public. It was a description of something larger that I wanted to write. Or so at the time I thought.

Read what you've actually written, I was told. As far as

we're concerned, this isn't just a long outline, it's a complete short novel in itself, and all that it needs is a few extra scenes here and there.

I reread *Journals of the Plague Years,* the manuscript of the short novel you have just read yourself with a few minor additions, and they were right. It *was* all there.

And so *Journals of the Plague Years* saw its first publication in *Full Spectrum* in 1988. It was critically well received. In the next five years, it was published in several other languages. In France and in Finland it has been used in AIDS education programs. It has, in certain circumscribed circles, become something of a classic.

And yet I was never quite satisfied.

Time passed, but the plague didn't. Time passed, and AIDS became more and more a subject of central cultural concern. Time passed, and friends died. Time passed, and millions of words about AIDS saw public print.

Time passed, and as it did, I felt more and more that *Journals of the Plague Years* needed to be published in a form that would be more permanent, that would reach a more general audience than the readership of an anthology of speculative fiction, no matter how successful.

I wanted *Journals of the Plague Years* published as a book, in other words.

This put me in something of a quandary.

Six years on, publishing perceptions had changed, ironically enough probably in part due to the publication of *Journals of the Plague Years* itself and its nomination for science fiction awards, and the chances were pretty good that now I could find a publisher for the very full-length novel I had written it as an outline for in the first place.

But I no longer wanted to write that book.

In retrospect, it seemed clear to me that fate, karma, commercial constraints, and subconscious forces had already combined, back in 1987, to cause me to write just about exactly what I should've written, namely *Journals of the Plague Years* as it appears in this book.

Rereading it, there's precious little that I would want to change, and expanding it to twice its size would, at least in the author's estimation, add little more than hot air.

Fortunately for me as the author, and I believe for you as the reader too, publishing perceptions have changed, and Bantam Books, the very publisher that could not see its way clear to publishing *Journals of the Plague Years* as a long book in 1987, now feels able to publish it as a shorter one in 1995.

This is just the way I wanted *Journals of the Plague Years* published, upon reflection, and so it should make me happy, and on the level of maintaining the work's literary integrity and allowing it the chance to reach a new audience, it does.

Yet on another level, it makes me sad.

For I cannot really avoid the realization that *Journals of the Plague Years* is now viable in book form because the matters that it deals with have, alas, become more central to our lives than ever they were in 1987, not less, so central that denial is no longer a viable psychic option.

The writer of speculative fiction dies a little whenever the passage of time eclipses one of his visions, but if ever there was a work of speculative fiction of mine that I *wanted* to see turned into a quaint, obsolete period piece, *Journals of the Plague Years* is surely it.

If we were emerging from the Plague Years it describes, rather than moving ever deeper into them, closer and closer to that tragic world of my imagining, then friends of mine who have died might still be alive. How few among you cannot say the same? In future years, how many fewer still?

The story that I wrote in 1987 begins with a fictitious retrospective introduction purportedly written in 2143 by a critic in a happier age looking back on the Years of the Plague.

"It was the worst of times, and it was the saddest of times," he writes.

Alas, in 1995, it seems painfully clear that those times are becoming more and more our own.

ABOUT THE AUTHOR

NORMAN SPINRAD is the internationally acclaimed author of sixteen novels including *Bug Jack Barron, The Iron Dream, Little Heroes,* and *Russian Spring* that have been translated into more than a dozen languages. He is also the author of numerous short stories and screenplays, is a political commentator, literary critic, and an occasional songwriter. Spinrad currently resides in Paris.